Hundred Shades of red

Robert Vermeer

Hundred Shades of Red

EROTIC THRILLER

Uitgeverij Aspekt

HUNDRED SHADES OF RED
© Robert Vermeer
© 2015 Uitgeverij ASPEKT
Amersfoortsestraat 27, 3769 AD Soesterberg, Nederland
info@uitgeverijaspekt.nl-http://www.uitgeverijaspekt.nl

Omslagontwerp: Mark Heuveling
Binnenwerk: Thomas Wunderink

ISBN: 9789461536082
NUR: 455

Alle rechten voorbehouden. Niets van deze uitgave mag worden verveelvoudigd, opgeslagen in een geautomatiseerd gegevensbestand of openbaar gemaakt, in enige vorm of op enige wijze, hetzij elektronisch, mechanisch, door fotokopieën, opnamen of enig andere manier, zonder voorafgaande toestemming van de uitgever.

Voorzover het maken van kopieën uit deze uitgave is toegestaan op grond van artikel 16B Auteurswet 1912 j° het Besluit van 20 juni 1974, St.b. 351, zoals gewijzigd bij het Besluit van 23 augustus 1985, St.b. 471 en artikel 17 Auteurswet 1912, dient men de daarvoor wettelijk verschuldigde vergoedingen te voldoen aan de Stichting Reprorecht (postbus 882, 1180 AW, Amstelveen). Voor het overnemen van gedeelte(n) van deze uitgave in bloemlezingen, readers, en andere compilatiewerken (artikel 16 Auteurswet 1912), dient men zich tot de uitgever te wenden.

Foreword

This erotic thriller is based on real events. For obvious reasons this book has been written under a pseudonym. The author-physician - endocrinologist - collaborated in 'difficult cases' with his brother, professor of psychology at the University of Amsterdam, during the period 1980-2002.

This story about a sin-laden, guilt-ridden relationship between two adults - brother and sister - laboriously established under the crafty direction of the husband who has a homo-erotic relationship with her brother, is based on testimonies of the woman and her husband during many therapeutic sessions where mostly only one of the partners was present. The testimonies have also been recorded electronically.

Although the story line is based on real events the author has chosen to tell the story as a novel (fiction) for the sake of the freedom it offers to the author. I hope you'll enjoy the book.

One thing I have learnt from my own patients and those of my brother: within the family sometimes things happen that even the most imaginative fiction writer could not have conceived.

The publisher is of course fully informed about the identity of the author and his brother, psychologist.

Finally I would like to offer my apologies to some readers for a number of rather graphic homo-erotic scenes. Regrettably this is almost unavoidable since the sexual relationship between the main characters Frans and his wife's brother, Hans, is the driving force behind the events.

Indispensable introduction
The biological background

In this true but 'blown-up' story in which a nice, decent woman ultimately succumbs to the manipulations of her husband to have intercourse with her own brother the question arises, 'How could it be that this 'respectable' woman was unable to resist this form of incest?' The answer only came to light in the mid-nineties and bears the name '**Genetic sexual attraction**', or GSA**.

Wikipedia says (abbr.): "**Genetic sexual attraction** is sexual attraction between close relatives, such as siblings, who first meet as adults, typically as a consequence of adoption. Although this is a rare consequence of adoptive reunions, the large number of adoptive reunions in recent years means that a large number of people are affected. If a sexual relationship is entered, it is known as incest."

It turns out that the greater the physical likeness between brother and sister the higher the percentage love affairs and the stronger the mutual attraction. In the extreme case brother and sister possess virtually identical DNA profiles, with the exception that the Y-chromosome is missing in the female.

In a study in which the researchers were shown the pictures of the persons involved they were able to predict with a high degree of accuracy which siblings had a sexual relationship. The greater the physical likeness the higher the probability, because in these cases the mutual sexual attraction was strongest.

For obvious reasons this phenomenon has not been sufficiently studied in siblings in the same family since in those cases 'sexual abuse' and 'depravity' could be deemed to be the primary cause.

Moreover, here the so-called Westermarck effect is the dominating factor, the phenomenon that children who live in close proximity become desensitized to later sexual attraction.

The phenomenon is called after the Swedish-Finnish anthropologist Edward Westermarck (see Wiki). In contradiction to Freud Westermarck posits that the incest taboo has arisen from the fact that family members have actually no sexual interest in each other and sex between family members is therefore unacceptable.

The Westermarck effect is not only present among family members, but also in other groups of children who have spent most of their youth together. For example a study on Israeli kibbutz's shows that of 3000 marriages only 14 (0.5 %) were between partners from the same group (Wiki).

What has the GSA to do with our story? Everything. Iris and her younger brother, Hans, closely resemble each other. You could almost say that Hans looked like the male replica of his sister. So, Iris, without having the slightest notion, is handicapped by the GSA effect. 'Subconsciously', physically, she feels erotically drawn to Hans. Her conscious 'I' (EGO), feminine chastity, and moral sense however exclude any erotic thought of physical intimacy, this in sharp contrast to her brother, who, under the influence of raging testosterone and completely under the spell of GSA is secretly madly in love with his beautiful sister and covets her in his sexual fantasies.

But GSA also exerts its influence on Frans, Iris' husband, who falls (sexually) in love with Hans, Iris' male replica.

This indirect influence of GSA on Frans is known as **shadow GSA,** but it almost always refers to 'attraction' by an individual of the opposite sex. The two most famous cases involve politics. Two Prime Ministers, Hans Wiegel of the Netherlands and Ariel Sharon of Israel lost their wives early in their marriage. Both, young, dashing, 'the most eligible widowers in town', remarried their wives' sisters, 'look-alikes'.

However in this chronicle the shadow GSA exerts its influence with regard to a person of the same sex (Hans attracts Frans). Frans sexual infatuation with Hans is the driving force of this story.

The annual celebration

1

Frans van Gaal, 23, tall, dark and boyish, in his fourth year of study at Delft Technical University, was in no mood to attend the anniversary of his student's union, the *Delftsche Studenten Corps.* He was still all cut up about the fact that Ingrid Weinberg had suddenly broken off their 2-year affair. The reason? He had been writing a half-finished autobiographical novel in the style of Marcel Proust in which the first-person narrator had a girl friend who bore some resemblance to Ingrid. Since Ingrid was ignorant about literature in general and Proust in particular there was no way he could make it clear to her that the characters in his book (including the narrator) had little to do with her or him, but were merely caricatures of reality, originating from the imagination of the author.

Ingrid was 'the prettiest girl in the classroom' as the (Dutch) saying goes, and the smartest. Tall, 1.80, extremely attractive, with her dreamy eyes, inviting look, wide red mouth and dimpled cheeks, even when she smiled at you ...

How did they meet. After a physics lecture, as they left the lecture theatre, she had smiled at him with a faint inviting smile and *that was it* ... She had picked him up, not the other way round. Frans, the womanizer, who at times had four girlfriends at a time, became outright monogamous.

They were not very close but they were a couple, went to the movies and concerts and on vacation together, but regrettably not to bed. *'Serious necking to climax'*, but no intercourse; that she didn't want before marriage. Did he love her? The question had never occurred to him, let alone the idea of marrying. One remark of hers was etched in his brain. They were on vacation in Paris. Both had very little money and they stayed in the Quartier Latin in a room like van Gogh's with a bare, sloping concrete floor, where someone had just committed suicide. On their first night they looked at the starry sky and he heard Ingrid dreamily remark," Later we 'll say, 'Oh, how poor we were, but how happy.'" But there was a snag. Not Frans, but Frits, a final-year chemistry student was her great love. But he had broken off the affair because she didn't want to fuck before marriage, she had told Frans. *Oh how sad, but am I lucky,* Frans had thought. Yes, Frans was deeply unhappy after the rift.

But as the French poet Lamartine said long ago, "*Plaisir d'amour ne dure q'un moment, chagrin d'amour aussi.* " Roughly translated : joys of love last only briefly, pangs of love too.

Indeed, fortunately, thanks to an event that would happen some weeks after the rift.

Frans *knew* he had to go to the party. He owed it to his debating society. But now for the first time without Ingrid. A dinner-dance: a partner at dinner, but who?

Frans, a bit ill at ease in his stiff tails opened the door of the cab and gallantly offered his hand when his 'partner at dinner' got in. The only thing he knew about her was that her father was a doctor. She looked pretty in her cream coloured evening dress in empire style with matching gloves and tiara. And she was spontaneous and lively.

It looked like a lustre instead of an annual celebration: fabulous. Ah, donations from alumni: captains of industry. No match for the fraternities of 'non-technical' universities, Frans reflected. The club, what a building, what luxury for those poor students! Fabulous orchestras, packed halls, oceans of champagne, mountains of truffles, with thousands of laughing faces among ten thousand red roses and precious furniture, rented, it is true, but still …

"Shall we dance?" That was the last thing Frans said to his partner at dinner. The dance floor was packed. The group was swinging. Suddenly he saw her …, on the dance floor. He was bewildered, instantly in love, mesmerized. Literally love at first sight, something he would never have thought possible. A perfect stranger, a girl no older than eighteen and his heart, no, his very being was on fire. The only thing he could do was stare, stare at her with bulging eyes, while he kept dancing close to her (Later she told him, "I thought 'Why is that creepy guy staring at me all the time.'")

Iris was slim, of average height and wore a light blue evening dress. She was stunningly beautiful, but the place was swarming with gorgeous women that night. Beautiful, lovely, enchanting. How can words describe a rose? How can words describe a woman who, just by her very looks, rattles you completely, puts you in a love daze?

The music stopped, couples left the dance floor. Frans noticed that the girl was accompanied by two boys, no older than seventeen, first-year students, friends, who, she later told him, were both madly in love with her.

When the music started Frans did something he would never have done otherwise. He got up, ignored his partner, walked up to the table where the girl was sitting and ask her for a dance. She looked at the boys askance, but got up at once. When the music stopped they went to the bar on the next floor, exchanged telephone numbers and addresses, chatted for a while, till she exclaimed, "Gosh, I must return to my friends." Frans, head over heels in love, went home straight away, not realizing he had ruined the dream night of his parents at table. Two weeks later, Frans, former womanizer, who always hated being introduced to potential parents-in-law, went to her father and said, "I'm in love with your daughter."

Like two drops of water

2

Iris was genetically photogenic. When she was six she won the Shirley Temple Award while she stayed with one of her English aunts in the Midlands, reputably the region where England's most beautiful women come from. When she was ten she was elected for a Coca Cola TV spot out of 50,000 girls; at fourteen during a flight from Schiphol to Paris her stepmother was accosted by a French movie director who offered a small part for her daughter in the comedy *Minot sur la plage*. Her stepmother had an uneasy feeling about it, but a year later she recognized his name as she went to see the movie out of curiosity. At fifteen she became a much sought-after cover girl. When she left high school at sixteen she enrolled at the famous Theatre School in Amsterdam and between times did very nicely as a freelance model. Because of her height (1.68 m) she wasn't tall enough to be a professional model. Iris was good-looking, but she was definitely no Doutzen Kroes [Holland's current top model]. What she lacked was that undefinable something, super-charisma, the trademark of a top model. In fact, Iris was, apart from her striking looks, an inconspicuous person, just the girl next door.

All 'parts' of her face and their ordering were 'perfect': the tip-tilted nose with the gentle tip, the large almond-shaped green-grey eyes with those incredibly long silken eyelashes that gave her a dreamy look, the full, red, pouting lips, the elegant jawline, the result of, what the English call, '*good bone structure*', the high intelligent eyebrows and, then, that particular flaw: crooked teeth, that gave her, when she talked or laughed, that unique charm of hers. The long auburn curly hair falling over her round forehead completed the picture of a modern Botticelli maiden.

But thousands of women meet this description and all are different, unique. Frans, who only fancied nice-looking girls, was stunned by her refined personality, her inner and outer beauty.

It figures, for doesn't Goethe's saying hold, "*Nichts ist drinnen, nichts ist drauszen, den was innen is ist auszen.*" (Roughly translated, *"nothing is on the inside, nothing is on the outside, for what is inside is outside."* Indeed, Iris' outer and inner beauty were closely intertwined.

Frans studied aerospace engineering and had a room in Delft (where the world renowned Delft technical university is located), but he also had a comfortable attic room at his parent's home in Amsterdam. He much preferred living in Amsterdam, so he was in fact a commuter. Iris lived with her parents in Amsterdam, a perfect match.

Her father was a civil servant with a modest income and the family with eight children (the eldest daughter had recently left the parental home) lived in a row house in the city's 'Old-South'. The father had remarried, a year after his first wife, Yvonne, had left him (see later). When Frans made his first entry into the parental home Iris' stepmother was ironing amidst a Jan Steen scene of quarrelling boys, aria's booming sisters who were clearing the table and poker playing men with big cigars. His first reaction when he saw his future mother-in-law was, '*Oh, what a nice, charming woman, so unassuming and sweet*'. But what struck him most were two things: Iris was by far the prettiest of the four sisters and she didn't look one bit like her father. '*How could such a beautiful girl be begotten by such an ordinary man?*'

Four sisters. Iris was the youngest. Karin, a studious type with owlish spectacles was one year older than Iris. Anna, not bad looking at all, was three years older than Iris and Tess, the eldest, with a big mouth and horse's teeth, had just been married.

Only three of the four brothers, who were still living with their parents, were present. Hans 11, and his elder brothers Frits and Jan, both with a pointed nose and sharp features, resembled each other as brothers do. Hans didn't look a bit like them. He was the spitting (male) image of Iris, with the same tip-tilted nose, the same striking almond-shaped eyes with long dark eyelashes and – amazingly - the same crooked teeth.

A freak of nature, Frank thought in wonderment. Even more mysterious was the fact that - as was discovered in the hospital much later - Iris and Hans shared the same rare blood group AB-, that occurs in only 0.5 % of the population. The rest of the offspring was O+ and A+, which occurs in more than 30 % of the population. Extreme freak of nature. The doctors were puzzled. The enigma of the slight genetic diversity in the DNA (genome), a condition almost comparable to that of identical twins, with as a consequence only slight physical differences, **apart from the enormous difference: gender.**

Many years later a family friend, Roel, gynaecologist, who was baffled by the biological resemblance between brother and sister (later in the story he plays a crucial role) speculated that if during the early foetal development the testis would have failed to produce testosterone, Hans would not have been born as a boy, but as a girl, Hansje (a Dutch name for a girl), with all the features of his sister, Iris, except that it would have been a matter of pseudo-hermaphroditism (hermaphroditism is when the individual has both a testis and ovaries).

On the outside Hans (Hansje) would then be fully a woman. However the abdomen would not contain ovaries, but a non-descended non-functional testis.

Fast forward

Many years later, when Frans and Iris separated, one of Iris' psychiatrists, Dr. Johan de Graaf, sent video material and DNA samples of Iris and Hans to the top GSA expert, Dr. M. Greenberg of the Department of Psychiatry and Anthropology of the University of London with the request to make a statistical estimate, on the basis of the degree of similarity, of the probability that, if (theoretically speaking) both would have been adopted in different families and would have met as adults, they would have entered into a romantic relationship.

The answer did not surprise Dr. de Graaf: 95 percent. When Iris learned of the result it was as if a heavy load had fallen off her shoulders: so it was not 'depravity' but a hereditary defect (GSA) that had made her so vulnerable to the wicked manipulations of her husband and brother.

Budding happiness

3

Frans had never introduced a girlfriend to his parents. But within a week they were playing bridge together. His parents were very happy with his choice. "Oh, what a lovely girl, so sweet and natural, but how young she is, "his mother said. The months that followed were the happiest of his life. They were inseparable, *Just had* to see each other every evening. Old friendships were neglected or broken.

Except for going to the movies, opera or a concert occasionally, their favourite occupation - certainly his - was sex. Usually in his attic room, with its own entrance, or, in the summer, in the bushes of Amsterdam park.

Oh, the excitement of deflowering a very young innocent girl - his own - and then as the pinnacle of his efforts of seduction to make her perform fellatio (a first time for him, too), while in the beginning she hardly dared to look at his member. On that memorable evening in his attic room Frans observed for the first time a special phenomenon: his penis hitting his abdomen like a metronome, as he stood naked while Iris, on her knees, was kissing his balls and more …

Later he would experience this phenomenon - the hallmark of supreme excitement - on several occasions, as recorded in later chapters.

Although neither Frans nor Iris said, "I love you." they knew that their love was a commitment, everlasting, eternal. Oh, how wrong intuition can be!

Frans had told her early on that they would get married right after his graduation. This was not a promise, merely stating a fact.

The real story starts only a few months after their marriage, three years after they first met.

After the first year the 'honeymoon' ('being over the moon') was over. A year before their marriage a curious event took place, the forerunner of future erotic developments.

Shorts and shorts

4

About a year before they got married, three years after they first met, two events took place, which, at least according to the opinion of their psychologist (see epilogue), were the first indications of Frans' erotic interest in Hans, Iris' male 'alter ego'.

It was in the midst of summer. Scene: Iris' paternal home, the landing on the first floor.

Hans, 13, in shorts, comes out of a room and slips past Frank. As always they don't exchange a word. Frans' hand shoots out to his fly. Hans darts off as if stung by a wasp and shouts, "Dirty bastard!" Frans wasn't even surprised. He was not in self-reflection. He wasn't horny, didn't fancy Hans, didn't even have the slightest interest in the boy. It just happened. Dimly, he did realize he would never have done it with any of the other brothers or with any other kid for that matter. *Strange.*

The next event is the precursor of later developments. The only time that Frans titillated Iris erotically before their marriage with something in which Hans was directly involved was when they were making love in the small side-room on the first floor of Iris' parental home on a sultry summer afternoon.

They had the house all to themselves (everyone had left, even the mother and Hans was just leaving).

The three sisters did the chores in turn, doing the laundry, ironing, etc. Everything was arranged on the notice board.

The three boys masturbated, of course, but whereas the two older boys ejaculated in their handkerchiefs which they usually washed out afterwards, Hans had the objectionable habit of coming in his underpants and just throwing the shorts in the laundry basket. All three sisters found it disgusting but were to prudish to confront Hans with it.

When Frans and Iris walked up the stairs, Hans, with a guilty, dazed look, darted past them downwards.

"I bet he has just jacked off," Iris whispered in Frans' ear. She walked straight towards the closet to inspect the laundry basket while Frans was undressing in the small bedroom. Iris lifted the lid of the laundry basket. The penetrating smell of fresh sperm hit her in her face. Oddly enough she was always nauseated by the sight and smell of a sticky handkerchief she sometimes found in the laundry basket, but not at the sight of Hans' dirty underpants. Then - like now - she felt butterflies in her stomach, with her heart beating faster and blood rushing to her cheeks.

Funny. She felt ashamed about these stupid titillating sensations (subtle GSA influence).

While making love Frans got a wild idea. Knowing they were all alone he stood and walked naked to the laundry basket, rummaged about for Hans' underpants and went back to join Iris. Without a word he began to fuck her anew holding Hans' underpants in his hand.

"Do you smell something?" he whispered while he pushed the shorts against her nose. Her physical reaction came as a surprise. She didn't say anything, wasn't moaning softly, but Frans suddenly felt her cunt contracting rhythmically, her cunt's muscles deeply massaging his penis, an unique phenomenon that - like a rearing cock - happens only during super horniness.

When Frans tried to push the sticky part against her mouth she pushed his hand away with a sharp movement. He knew he'd gone too far ...

When they were close to orgasm Frans pushed the white stuff against her swollen nipple. "You feel it, darling, his seed?"

At that moment she came, a long, shaking, intense orgasm, while she seemed unaware of Frans kissing her with his mouth full of Hans' seed.

Only a bit later when Frans found her in the bathroom rinsing her mouth he suspected that she had known all along that she had gotten Hans' sperm in her mouth and perhaps swallowed some of it.

Afterwards not a word was spoken about this incident. Later Frans was a bit puzzled. He didn't have any conscious erotic interest in the boy and had - except for his own sperm - never tasted seed before. Maybe it was only the exciting idea of disconcerting the sister with her favourite brother's dab. Frans had been 'pleasantly surprised' that Iris had become so excited (her vagina's reaction told it all), but he had, of course, not the faintest notion that a biological influence lay at the bottom of it: GSA, genetic sexual attraction.

Two milestones

5

The family tragedy had its roots in two crucial events that determined the homo-erotic relation between Frans and Hans.

The first experience took place a few months after their wedding. Frans and Iris lived in a rented room in Delft. Poverty, academic poverty, for Frans was working on his PhD.

That single room, four by five meters, served as bedroom, dining room, sitting-room and study. The furniture was sparse: a wall bed, a sofa, a narrow coach near the window and a small dining table with four kitchen chairs. Before Hans stayed over for the weekend the two other brothers, Frits and Jan, had been invited on earlier occasions to stay the night.

When they had a guest Iris didn't want Frans to sleep with her because she knew it would end in their having sex and that she definitely didn't want to happen. So, Frans was forced to sleep snuggled up against the boy's back on the narrow couch. No problem. He was young and slept like a log. And not the slightest paedophile or homophile emotion or thought with Frits or Jan.

But with Hans it was totally different. It started at eleven: children's bedtime!

Like his two brothers Hans undressed while Iris discreetly turned away. Only now with Hans Frans felt an indefinable erotic tingling ('*Oh, how exciting!*' His flesh would have exclaimed if it were articulate), just because of the fact that Hans would stand naked for a few seconds in the presence of his sister. Frans shot a glance at Hans' infantile peter with its oversized foreskin. It was for Frans an electrifying, delicious moment.

The lights went out. By the audible slow, deep breathing Frans knew that Iris had immediately fallen asleep.

Frans, snuggled up against Hans' back, felt his nose touching Hans' neck.

Then something very strange happened. Something he had never experienced before or since.

His breathing carried on like a pair of bellows, very deep and especially very audible, almost loud in the stillness of the night. He tried to suppress it. In vain. Did he experience something, was he horny, did he have an erection? No, only this absurd loud deep breathing over which he had absolutely no control.

"Stop panting like that, I can't sleep," Hans snapped. The strange panting continued unabated.

Deeply annoyed Hans turned around 180 degrees, his head at the foot.

At about five Frans awoke. It was already getting lighter in the room. Iris and Hans were fast asleep. Without thinking Frans doubled up, opened the button of Hans' pyjama and looked at his white little Willie. Impulsively he planted a butterfly kiss on the child's peter. The moment his head hit the pillow he was gone.

Of course, later it all became clear to him: his doglike panting at the close physical presence of Hans was the absolute proof of the enormous erotic attraction the kid exerted on him. At least on that night, in that situation. Since that experience, however, Hans had completely vanished from Frans' radar screen.

******

The second experience about a year later was decisive.

Frans had bought his first motorcycle a few months ago, the BMW R100. He was proud as a peacock and very pleased. A fantastic machine. Iris and he had been to the Ardennes with it. A monster of an engine, not to be compared to the Berini M48, a moped with the characteristics of a light motorcycle. Hans had asked if he could ride pillion sometimes. Sure, next weekend, Frans had promised.

It was a perfect summer afternoon, 30 degrees, calm, with a clear blue sky. Hans ran out of the front door and jumped behind him while Frans was waiting with throbbing engine.

It gave him a calm, pleasantly excited feeling, a sense of freedom, to be alone with Hans for the first time in all those years. Frits, Hans' brother, had gone with him before but that was totally different. They rode to the Amsterdamse Bos [bos=woods], an enormous park of some 1000 hectares in Amstelveen [one of Amsterdam's suburbs] with sloping meadows dotted with groups of trees, small lakes, playing fields, hockey fields and, of course, the famous manmade rowing course, where the World championships were held in 1977.

Frans stopped at the top of a tall sloping hill. They were all by themselves. Far away you could see people no larger than dolls barbecue, playing badminton, sunbathing, just walking about.

No-one paid the slightest attention to them. Hans and Frans, sitting on a wooden bench under a shady oak chatted about mopeds, motorcycles, scouting and vacations. Suddenly, without premeditation Frans asked about girls and when he saw Hans blush he asked him about wet dreams and masturbation. All without conscious design. "Masturbation? What's that?"

"Frigging," Frans said, as he put his hand on the forbidden zone and started rubbing gently. Later neither Frans nor Hans could recall who had opened his fly. As Frans stooped he noticed that his peter had lost its childlike character, as befits an adolescent (15). The next moment his peter became bigger and harder against the greedy movements of Frans' tongue.

"No, not here," Hans breathed, as he looked uneasily at the trippers in the distance. Frans stopped, vaguely surmising that these words held a sweet promise.

When they arrived home they found an empty house, except for Iris, who greeted them as she was peeling string beans. "Back so soon? Did you have a nice time? Did you enjoy the ride, Hans?"

After some chit-chat Hans and Frans went upstairs to the 'boys room'. The room had casement doors to a tiny balcony. This front room was separated from the backroom by a narrow 'storeroom' with an opening to the front room and a door to the landing.

No word was spoken. Hans stood with his back to the wall and let Frans do his thing. Frans kneeled, opened his fly and began blowing him. Frans' tongue and lips made gentle movements, as he wanted to enjoy the experience as long as possible. Minutes passed. Iris, a bit surprised at the long silence called out, without a trace of suspicion, "What are you both doing up there?"

Just at that moment Hans came. While Frans felt the blobs of seed gush jerkily into his greedy mouth he heard the impatient tittup of high heels in the hall downstairs. He didn't panic for he thought in the glow of pleasure that there would still be plenty of time.

It seemed as if time stood still: everything appeared to happen in slow motion. Iris stood at the foot of the stairs and called again, "What are you both doing for Christ's sake? Are you coming down, Frans? Tea is ready?"

Frans 'knew' Iris wouldn't come upstairs. Still he was a bit anxious. He wanted to pull back, but Hans pushed his belly forward and his hand against Frans' head, groaning silently, while his glans kept throbbing against Frans' palate and semen kept gushing. Seconds later Frans heard footsteps on the stairs. The sticky stuff kept coming. Then suddenly, total relaxation, while a deep sigh escaped from Hans' lips. Frans stood, his mouth full of seed.

Just the very moment the door opened Hans darted off to the 'storeroom'. Iris, who saw Frans in a state of panic, called out, rushing towards him, "What's wrong, what's wrong, dear?"

Panic makes you sly. He beat his hand against his chest as if there was something wrong with his heart and darted to the mini-balcony, gasping for air. "I'm not feeling well, but I'll be fine in a minute. I just need a bit of fresh air!" Frans shouted in total confusion, as Iris, greatly concerned, put her hand on his shoulder as he stooped over the railing.

Frans managed to reassure Iris and from the stairs he heard her calling out, "Where is Hans?"

"In the attic, I think."

That was a close thing!

His fear, of course, was that Iris would smell her brother's semen.

Homo, bisexual or 'mono'?

6

Frans, analytical by nature, wondered if he was bisexual, despite his exclusive interest in women. Fairly well informed about psychoanalytical concepts as 'repression' and the subconscious he decided to have himself tested at the University hospital in Leyden with regard to his sexual orientation.

While the person looks at hetero, homo and 'pedo' sex-video's the reaction is objectively determined by means of a variety of techniques, including brain scans, skin resistance, and penis volume measurements (so-called plethysmography).

A month later the results were available. In lay terms it amounted to this: sex orientation exclusively hetero. Homo interest negative, that is, physical aversion to men. Pedo interest restricted to pretty adolescents with girlish looks, so, 'beautiful, effeminate boys'.

These are as rare as a supermodel in a supermarket.

Frans was a bit confused: Hans was a pretty boy - almost too pretty for a male - but definitely not effeminate. A normal boy, like his brothers and friends.

The only thing Frans could think of was that perhaps his striking resemblance to his sister Iris had something to do with this. Or, perhaps it was just his 'beauty', although it was not 'effeminate'. Or, perhaps, his personality, his 'persona'. Reincarnation perhaps? Perhaps Hans had been his wife in a previous life. Such idiotic ruminations sometimes floated in his confused mind.

Iris too - like everybody else - was aware of this close likeness between herself and Hans. Once she told Frans that, when she came home from skating in the Vondelpark (Amsterdam's Hyde Park) in the middle of winter and caught a glimpse of herself in the hall mirror with glowing cheeks and woolly hat, she thought for a fraction of a second that she was seeing Hans.

The explanation of Frans' erotic interest in Hans as a kind of side effect of GSA, known as **shadow GSA** came only many years later.

***

The memorable summer's day in the Amsterdam Bos (park) was the beginning of a secret sexual relation between Frans and Hans that would last over the years, even when Hans was married.

Since Frans and Iris lived in Delft in those days and stayed every weekend at Iris' 'family home' in Amsterdam, there was plenty of opportunity for oral sex.

Frans and Iris slept in the 'in-between room' on the first floor, that was open to the boys room where the three boys slept on divan beds. Hans' bed was closest to the opening. Frans, checking his Seiko with the light-emitting hands would slip out of bed at three o'clock sharp, and walk to the boys room, kneel at Hans' bed where - often - Hans lay already waiting for him with an erection. Oh, the sense of time of youth!

Both his brothers slept like a log. In the filtered light of the streetlamp the medium-sized hard penis was clearly visible. Frans enjoyed looking but regretted that most of the glans was covered by the narrow foreskin that also impeded full expansion during erection.

What had struck him from the start was that instead of being darker - more pigmented - than the rest of the body it was just as white.

The blow job never lasted more than three minutes. Still savouring the pungent taste of semen, licking his lips, Frans would sneak back to the poky little room where he promptly fell asleep next to Iris.

During the weekends and sometimes during the week there were plenty of opportunities for sex: in the cellar, in the evening under a footbridge in the Vondelpark (Amsterdam's Hyde park), in Frans' car and on rare occasions in a motel.

No one had any inkling, except, perhaps, Iris' eldest sister, Tess, who, when one day Frans entered the living room after coming in his underpants during a blow job in the Vondelpark, made the quizzical remark, "It smells like milk here." He had felt a bit uncomfortable.

A remarkable experience that offered Frans the certitude that the fellatio pleasure was not caused by a penis - any penis - but only by Hans' penis and so by Hans' personality was the following.

When Frans one day wanted to do his particular act at three o'clock he found Hans' bed empty. As a surrogate he went to Frits who was soundly asleep. Frans pulled his peter from out of his pyjama and started to blow him .The erection came promptly while Frits was lying on his back. He seemed to enjoy it. In the dim light of the streetlamp Frits' peter was clearly visible: in all respects identical to Hans' penis, including the narrow foreskin and the lack of pigmentation. After seconds Frans stopped. It left him cold.

He thought it a valuable lesson. It taught him that it was not about a penis, but only Hans' penis.

Much later (see epilogue) he told this experience to his psychiatrist, commenting, "I was obviously in love with his penis, only his."

The psychiatrist, wiping his glasses, had answered with perfect logic," So, you were in love with your brother-in-law." Frans had blushed. Madly in love with a man, how 'homo' it sounds.

He had countered, "Yes, you could say that, 'sexually in love'."

One thing was clear to him after the hospital testing and his own experience: he was no 'homo' but a 'mono', in love with a single person of the same gender, Hans.

During the first two years they had sex, according to Frans' estimate, some three hundred times, with Hans nearly always in the passive role.

Interlude

7

Although the next episode is only tangentially related to our chronicle of sexual depravity, including incest, it should be mentioned in passing, since it throws some light on the erotic effect that the nature of a penis aroused in Iris.

Frans and Iris had met Henk and Sietske at a party. They hit it off right from the start. He was a psychiatrist, she had worked as an X-ray technician before her marriage.

Henk was rather short, with an infectious laugh, a great sense of humour and always talked with his hands like a full-blooded Italian.

Lively fellow, but very *sympathico*. Although he scored a mere six on the sex-appeal scale Iris felt attracted to him by the warmth of his sparkling personality. Iris thought his falsetto voice rather charming. Sietske was pale, thin as a rake, with juvenile breasts and even a wide scar on her cheek: also not worth more than a mere six.

She told that sometimes when she was scrubbing the windows outside her house a visitor would ask: "Is the mistress at home?"

But, oh, how funny and sensitive she was and - for Frans - very sexy!

The first time they went out together they had a lovely meal in the Oesterbar at the Leidseplein, Amsterdam's Piccadilly Centre and danced all through the night in a trendy disco in Amsterdam's famous red-light district.

Somewhat unsteady they made their way home, under the influence of wine and the intimacy of their newly found friendship.

Frans and Sietske were steadily falling back as they dashed into a doorway at every opportunity to kiss and touch. It was the first time since he met Iris that he had kissed another woman.

That was the beginning of a quadrilateral relationship that would last for several months; always on weekends, when Frans and Iris stayed with them.

For this chronicle the three relevant features of this partner-swapping were the following:

- Every weekend Frans could decide whether to stay with Sietske and Henk or at Iris 'parental home'. The last would have been his 'natural choice' as it offered him the opportunity to give in to his unnatural habit, the nightly fellatio. It had become a kind of addiction. Iris would always comply. Since the beginning the choice was easy: spending the night with Sietske, the woman he had fallen in love with, was far preferable to three minutes oral sex. There was so much warmth, love and intimacy! As a welcome side-effect it reassured him about his sexual orientation: strictly hetero, clearly.

- It was a gradual process, but after the first excitement had worn off Iris became more and more reluctant to sleep with Henk. The reason? His too small peter, as she later told Frans. It gave her little pleasure during intercourse and she found the sight of his Willie aesthetically more and more unpleasant.

This negative experience was perhaps the subconscious stimulus for her secret female interest in, what she called in her diary, '*penis beauty*', not merely penis size. The only thing that excited Iris in *Playboy Magazine* and other sex magazines that Frans occasionally brought home were the peters and fantasying about performing fellatio on an oversized penis.

Even after her marriage Iris had slept a few times in the small 'in-between room' on her own, and when early one morning Iris left her 'closet room' via the boys room Hans was lying on his back with a morning erection, whereby his penis stuck out above his tight underpants. She was amazed how much it had grown since she saw it ages ago. *Oh, what a pity his glans isn't visible,* a small voice of her flesh whispered. She felt her pussy getting wet and butterflies fluttering around her nipples when she – fooling herself – went back from the bathroom to her bedroom to choose another lipstick. Oh, how Iris could fool herself without being aware of it. Her lower 'I' concluded with impeccable feminine good taste that Hans hard cock was more attractive than Frans' and a thousand times more attractive than Henk's penis. For days the alluring picture of Hans' erection appeared in her wet dreams in which she shamefully swallowed the 'delicious semen' of her favourite brother. Oh, the shame and self-loathing at the awakening!

- Just as an adolescent thinks that he/she is the only one who masturbates, so Iris thought that she was the only woman with a perverse interest in exciting peters. Her shame became less embarrassing when her best friend, Thea, compared it to the interest of men in (pretty) breasts . After her visit to a 'sex palace' in Antwerp with Thea, where a 'beauty contest' was held in which the (female) audience could select the winner by smartphone from 30 hard cocks protruding from round holes, she felt much better about it.

    She lost her sense of shame permanently when, in 2012, she heard her favourite author, Connie Palmen, tell in a talk-show that she had originally spoken of 'his wonderful penis' in the manuscript of her biography of her late husband, the well-known politician Hans van Mierlo. Ultimately she had decided to change it to "his wonderful hands'. So, she was clearly not the only woman who could appreciate the beauty of a peter. *But her own brother's …*

Henk had taken lots of pictures of Iris without her being aware of it. Those were the nicest. With the exception of one picture taken in their back garden, her face dark as a thundercloud. Frans had never seen her like that before.

Something serious must be the matter. The truth had to be dragged out of her: she had felt very guilty for two reasons, three, really. First, because committing adultery - that it was, wasn't it - was prohibited by the Catholic faith: an abomination in God's eyes.

Moreover, just the very thought of what her parents (her father and step-mother) would think of her when they knew … Finally, the idea that her biological mother, Yvonne, would see everything from heaven what she was up to.

All three of them could argue for hours: to no avail. Her deep sense of guilt and shame remained despite her knowledge that God would forgive her if she would go to confession and show real remorse and despite Frans' rational argument with regard to her parents that ignorance is bliss.

"Women," he sighed inwardly, "stupid, irrational creatures."

These three factors are mentioned because in the hidden depths of Iris' soul they played a significant role in later developments in which Hans, her brother, was closely involved.

Shortly after the garden picture the affair came - due to Iris - to an abrupt end, to Frans' and Sietske's deep sorrow, friends who had grown very fond of each other.

Early GSA effects between Hans and Iris

8

Prologue

Almost time for the well-wishers to leave the *Rotterdam*. Yvonne, thirty-eight, just remarried, leaves for America with her new husband, John Slater and her youngest child from a large family, Hans. By boat, as she has a panic fear of flying.

The whole family was gathered in the lounge, except Yvonne's ex and her eldest daughter who was furious that she left her whole family in the lurch to run off with a millionaire. The quay is full of well-wishers. The children in the lounge just can't say goodbye to their mother and to Hans, a sweet little child who only laughs and coos.

The steam whistle of the *Rotterdam* blares the first signal. All non-passengers must leave the ship. After a few minutes the second shrill whistle. A final embrace, a last kiss. The children find it terrible that they may perhaps never see their mother again.

Iris, eight, is totally distraught, her eyes filled with tears, as she fondly holds Hans for the last time. Hans laughs and coos …

'She's like a mother who must give up her child,' the steward in white summer uniform thinks, as he discretely watches the little scene.

****

Six years later Yvonne, Hans' mother, dies of breast cancer. The child is dumped by his step-father, fortunately in the lap of Hans' family in Amsterdam, to the great joy of the father, brothers and sisters, but especially to Iris, who is delirious with joy. At the time Hans is eight, Iris fourteen, when Iris takes her favourite brother lovingly into her arms at Schiphol airport.

"Hans is the very image of Iris at that age," auntie Loes says, as she watches the little scene." Could be a twin: same eyes, same upturned nose, same mouth, same dimpled cheeks when he laughs, even the same birthmark. Very odd."

******

With the two other brothers, who were also much younger than Iris, she never had an erotic encounter or thought, but with Hans it was totally different. Of course neither of them knew that they were the victim of a genetic condition GSA because of their close DNA relationship. As a background of later developments encouraged and initiated by Frans, some typical incidents must be mentioned that took place in the period before Iris met Frans until their marriage.

Two years after Hans returned to the family following the death of his mother, Yvonne.

Hans was ten at the time, Iris sixteen. Iris looked more mature than her age, while Hans was always estimated a bit younger than his age.

He was delicate and a bit shorter than his peers. He was also a bit more immature than most boys his age. At the time Iris slept apart from her sisters in a small side-room on the first floor of the family home. On Sunday morning Hans would slip into Iris' bed and promptly doze off to sleep. One day he started playing with her half-exposed breast and showed serious erotic interest, a bit like very young children sucking their big toe. At the same time she felt a semi-erection rubbing against her belly. She should have pushed him roughly away at that moment. Instead she only stopped him after she let him do his thing, as he loosened the strap of her rose chiffon nightgown, fondled her exposed breast and started to suck her breast innocently like a newborn baby. Oh, the delicious sensations of the moment, the butterflies in her stomach, around her nipple!

Although 'innocent' she did notice his red glowing cheeks and his quick-tempered desire to continue when she pushed him away. Iris felt very guilty afterwards, for she realized that a limit had been crossed, but especially because she found his 'quest' so exquisitely exciting. Long after Iris had brusquely ordered Hans out of the room her nipples remained rosy and swollen, while she was staring on her back to the ceiling. **GSA**, but, of course, she'd no idea.

**

To illustrate the 'closeness' and natural intimacy between Iris and Hans the boat trip on Lake Christallina in Canton Ticino, Switzerland, where Iris, Hans and other members of the family were on vacation, is worth mentioning.

In the spacious motorboat with outboard engine in which the family and other tourists had seated themselves Iris and Hans were sitting intimately together.

Herr Kauffmann and his wife were watching the little scene with rising wonderment. Hans and Iris were so physical, so intimate, the way they touched each other, embraced, laughed and almost kissed under the nose, that Herr Kauffmann couldn't help remarking to his wife, "You would almost think those two are having an affair." Yes, they did everything a pair of lovers would do in public. Herr Kauffmann watched with fascination, but the rest of the family obviously thought it perfectly normal, as nobody paid the least attention to those two.

**

The first incident in which GSA was clearly involved should be mentioned.

It concerns a forbidden fruit: not an apple but a banana.

Older sisters are always busy taking care of their younger brothers. One day when Hans was twelve years old he had sustained an ugly gash on his knee when he ran into another cyclist as he ran a traffic-light. Since the neglected injury started to discharge pus, the wound had to be cleaned daily and the bandage changed. Hans sat on the dinner table, while Iris, in kneeling position, treated the injury. She had felt awkward on a number of occasions when she caught a glimpse of his peter in the leg of his shorts. One day - the last - she noticed to her alarm that he had an erection and she caught herself feeling sorry that this would be the last time. For days salacious images of this forbidden fruit loomed up in her (wet) dreams which she could clearly recall. *Oh, the shame and self-hatred at the awakening*!

Hans' erection was for a reason. At twelve he had already ejaculations and became interested in sex (porno, girls, etc.). And Iris was the favourite of his erotic fantasies and wet dreams. This is what happened.

Iris wore a low-cut floral summer dress without a bra. To Hans' secret delight he could freely enjoy the sight of Iris' half-exposed breasts from his high position. The images of her nipple and areola etched in his brain fanned the fires of his newly discovered self-abuse to the stage of delirium.

Both Hans and Iris experienced a flurry of secret excitement when one week later the wound again started to suppurate and would require another round of sisterly care. Iris in her flimsy summer dress was totally unaware of the fact that her Renoir-like bosom was exposed to Hans' hungrily staring eyes. Iris, who in vain tried not to look, couldn't help repeatedly casting fleeting glances at his purple pulsing glans so near her face, as her vulva became moist, her nipples glowed and electricity rippled through her sinful flesh. Iris, who in her innocence had no notion about the cause of her brother's lewdness, just thought, 'Oh, boys will be boys.'

On day 3 of the second round things really got out of hand. Hans, already excited by the sight of Iris-half-bared breasts, suddenly noticed that Iris was staring like mesmerized in the leg of his shorts He noticed that she was a bit flustered.

The mere fact that he knew that his sister was staring at his hard peter had an unprecedented effect on him: a spontaneous orgasm, purely mental. He started visibly.

In a desperate attempt to stop the seminal discharge he threw his legs in the air, which resulted in his hard dick emerging from his pulled leg and the semen squirting against her neck and lower. It was a moment of total confusion and embarrassment for both. No word was spoken. Iris stood and left the room. Hans went to the toilet to wipe off the worst.

But the job had to be finished. Iris had no choice but to call him back and let him sit on the table. After bandaging the wound she went straight to her small bedroom where she lay on her back, mentally exhausted. She wasn't angry with Hans, after all it was *her* fault, not his. She felt deeply ashamed that he had caught her staring into his leg, though it had been unintentional. One thing was sure: Hans was erotically dangerous, very dangerous.

Despite this painful incident they stayed close and after some weeks all awkwardness and aloofness had evaporated from their close relationship. But the turning point came suddenly. With the other members of the family they were watching TV. Hans was sitting on Iris' lap, blowing bubble gum, moving his legs, as kids do. Suddenly Iris was flooded by an acute sexual urgency that far exceeded sisterly love. She knew it was wrong when she felt these exciting sensations in her genital area. What she didn't know - or didn't realize – was that these sexual sensations were caused by his rhythmic leg movements subtly transmitted by her thighs to her vulva.

On the other hand, as Iris' psychiatrist observed many years later, the earth must be properly prepared for the bush of the forbidden fruit to take root. **GSA:** at the time the undiscovered fertilizer. The combination of his rhythmic tramp and GSA: oh, what a poisonous mix!

In a kind of moral panic she pushed him away and went to the kitchen for a mug of Rooibos tea. It was the last time she allowed herself close physical contact with her beloved little brother.

The next day, while she was watching her favourite soap on her own, Hans, chewing popcorn, flopped on her lap. Angrily she pushed him away, like the proverbial father pushing away his too attractive fourteen-year old daughter flopping on his lap.

Deeply hurt, feeling rejected, Hans shut himself up in his own private world for weeks before he could face up to the new reality: being treated by Iris the same way as his two older brothers.

The last straw

The last straw that drove Iris to distance herself emotionally from Hans to the level of a 'normal' brother-sister relationship came suddenly towards daybreak.

But for a better understanding of the situation it is necessary to mention an earlier incestuous relation with his sister Anna, two years older than Iris.

One afternoon Hans was jerking himself off in his room when Anna opened the door and stood in front of him. Startled, he held his French textbook in front of his peter.

"Show it, show it, or else I'll tell mother," Anna threatened excitedly, as she tore the book from his hands.

His exposed hard penis close to an orgasm swayed like a palm tree in a sandstorm. Mesmerized Anna stood, bended over him. Just like in the incident with Iris, Hans had at that instant a spontaneous ejaculation, so, without touching. Just because his sister was staring at his cock in a state of great agitation.

Instead of leaving the room in a state of shock, Anna lovingly wiped off the seed from his shorts and thighs with her handkerchief and even touched his penis with her fingers, a loving gesture full of promise and the beginning of a forbidden relationship resulting in deep-throat sex and even - shortly after Anna and her fiancé had moved into their flat - in intercourse, initiated by his older sister of course.

It went on for some time until Frans put a stop to it at one of the monthly dance parties at the 'family home'.

Since Frans and Anna sometimes flirted innocently and as she thought 'he knew everything', she asked him one day, "You can't get pregnant from the semen of a thirteen-year old boy, can you?"

Frans was a bit surprised by the question and said, "Of course you can, sperm is always fertile." She looked a bit startled but said nothing.

The point of this digression is to show how Hans in his bottomless ignorance about the psychology of women thought that all sisters were like Anna: open to fellatio with their little brother under the right circumstances. How stupid a kid can be! Iris was totally different from Anna, a bit of a tart, who even had sex with Frans' brother, Albert, despite being engaged, when he stayed at the 'family home' for a month because of his studies.

Subconsciously this experience with Anna had contributed to Hans' completely wrong assessment on that fatal night.

These were the circumstances.

As usual Iris slept in the 'in-between room', as the reader knows, the poky little room between the girls' room at the back and the boys' room. An opening, partly covered by a curtain, opened to the boys' room. But on this hot summer evening the opening was unobstructed.

As mentioned earlier there were three divan beds in the boys' room. Hans' bed was nearest to the opening.

It was at dawn. The boys' room was dimly lit, while a nightlight lit Iris' den in a soft reddish glow.

Hans was lying on his back masturbating, his underpants pulled down, when he suddenly noticed that Iris was watching, wide-eyed, her head slightly raised from the pillow. Since he only knew WOMAN through Anna, his naughty sister, he thought all women were like her. In his excitement, 'knowing' she felt like having sex, he whispered her name. The two other boys were fast asleep. He saw she was startled. Her head fell back on the pillow and she pretended to be sleeping, inwardly deeply ashamed that she had been caught in the act and in a state of utter confusion.

Hans didn't think any further, he acted. He had seen his sister awake and now she was pretending to be asleep. That could only mean one thing: she wanted to be captured. *The idiot.* Naked (in summer the boys slept wearing only their tight underpants) he walked up to her bed. Again he whispered her name. No response. In his lewdness and naivety he stooped over her and pushed his glans against her lips as he fondled her breast through the flimsy Lolita.

In her shame and panic she reacted like a rabbit in the headlights: she stayed immobile, frozen, pretending to be fast asleep, until she felt to her dismay his glans pushing against her gums.

Instinctively, she pretended to wake up abruptly. She played the role to perfection. Confused, she sat up, blinking her eyes, as if being shaken out of a profound sleep.

Hans felt the spontaneous semen discharge coming and fled, his hand held hollow under his glans, to his bed, where he caught the milky stuff in his discarded underpants.

For Iris this traumatic experience was the last drop. Never, never again she wanted anything to do with Hans with even a hint of intimacy or eroticism. This was the last straw! Incest with Hans, like her slutty sister, Anna, Frans had told her about? *Never ...*

The seismograph

9

Frans and Iris were crazy about sex, especially on long drives, like on the day they went to Maastricht for TEFAF, the world's most important antique fair, although they didn't have a red cent. They started to fool around the moment they hit the highway.

"Will you kiss me," he asked, touching her thigh and instinctively glancing in the 'rear-view' mirror.

"I see little big man is ready for immediate attention, "Iris said, opening his fly. Lovingly he cast a casual glance at her head in his lap.

When he was sufficiently stimulated she sat upright and unbuttoned her blouse. And Frans? One eye on the road, one eye on her bosom.

"Take it off, darling,"

"Should I?"

"Do it."

Just at the moment she took off her blouse a police car appeared out of nowhere.

Frans laughed nervously when the police passed without even looking up. This made it all the more exciting.

"Shall I tell you a story, darling?" He could make her horny as hell with his stories, especially when they were based on real events.

"If you want to, "Iris said, spreading her legs and lowering the back.

Perverse fantasies like lesbian love or 'woman and dog' were fine, but Iris found real-life stories the most exciting, especially sex involving Anna, her naughty sister, and Frans' brother, Albert, or her brother, Hans.

Even when horny Frans had this special gift to see things from a certain distance - like from a helicopter - a bit like Marcel Proust or Aldous Huxley in literary form.

While he fingered Iris he began with a fantasy. The reaction of her vagina scored a mere six. Her sister's relationship with his brother (see above) scored a seven on a ten point scale. But to his delight the stories about Anna and her brother Hans a ten! His best calibration instrument was his forefinger deep in her moist vagina. Just like a seismograph registers the seismic vibrations, his finger was able to feel the slightest contractions of her vagina muscles. Only when Iris was 'super-horny' her vagina muscles came to life, while her external labia swelled up to the size of flapjacks (this comes up again later), two phenomena he had never seen in any other woman before or since.

His calibration instrument registered flawlessly: mighty waves of sexual ecstasy swept over his finger making his other instrument almost explode. *His own wife excited by her brother, the lad he was sexually in love with!* Wow, what a discovery. It was like reading the most hidden thoughts, to register forbidden desires she would never admit to anyone, not even to herself. His forefinger was as a lie-detector, a brain scanner. He almost felt like Freud as he ejaculated deep into her pretty head.

Nothing could excite Frans more than the thought of the next step: to turn his fantasy about sex between Iris and Hans into reality. What seemed like a chimera yesterday might perhaps become reality! But the next moment common-sense prevailed: Iris was far too square for things like that. Her moral compass was too steadfast.

Frans moral compass was steadfast too, but the needle - represented by his penis - was not directed towards the north, but upwards, so, in the wrong direction. In other words: with regard to sex Frans was totally unscrupulous.

The cassette recorder

10

Since you, dear reader, are not just reading this book out of sensationalism, but because you're intrigued by the psychological interactions and the emotional life of the main characters, it is relevant as an introduction to this chapter to present a piece of 'medical diagnostics'. As mentioned in the epilogue Iris sought psychiatric help because of the heavy mental burden due to the incestuous experiences (see later). Her science-oriented psychiatrist asked Iris if she would be willing to participate as a 'special test subject' in a fMRI-study (functional MRI scan) conducted by the world-famous Dr. Pek van den Andel (see Wiki) at the University of Groningen. The experimental design was as follows:

The subject lies in the (confined) MRI machine and is brought to a state of extreme sexual excitement by ultrasonic waves directed at (in women) the labia and clitoris. The fMRI registers the blood flow intensity in the so-called prefrontal cortex, the brain area responsible for 'monitoring' behaviour and suppressing unwanted emotions, behaviours and utterances. Normal individuals show no changes in the blood flow of this area under these conditions.[1]

---

[1] It concerns especially the Brodmann areas 9 and 46. Dr. Pek van den Andel of the University of Groningen is the pioneer of MRI research

Hypersensitive individuals, characterized by the fact that they are very easily brought under hypnosis, like Iris, turn out to have a **diminished** blood flow of the prefrontal cortex during sexual hyper stimulation, resulting in a temporary disinhibition of unwanted behaviour (inclusive utterances).

This decreased blood flow of the prefrontal cortex during maximal erotic stimulation by means of ultrasonic vibrations was established in Iris by fMRI recordings.

Since this area is also responsible for the so-called working memory and selective attention, this explains why Iris later had no recall of all the crazy things she had shouted in her 'sexual trance' on that fateful evening. At least, the memory was as shadowy as that of a dream.

The events of the evening in question were as follows.

Frans was - to use a medieval image - not only a gladiator (his penis the sword) on the snow-white battlefield of the sexes, but also a troubadour (trobar means in *Occitan* (old French) 'to find', to 'think up').

This combination enabled him to subject any woman - including his own - to his wildest desires and lusts in bed, to impale her with his sword.

Iris enjoyed his randy stories, varying from bound women with Dobermans in a sex palace to sex scenes of Hans with his sister Anna. With the latter he was not generous, perhaps once every couple of weeks, to keep the theme fresh and exciting.

---

of 'sex in the MRI scanner'. For this he received the IG Nobel prize in Stockholm, given for studies 'that first make you laugh and later make you think.'

Frans had planned to drive her wild with desire by stories about Hans and Anna Hans had told him, on this evening with the hidden cassette recorder intended for Hans' hungry ears. Iris, in her naivity, didn't suspect anything about the sex relationship between Frans and Hans, despite all the intimate stories Hans apparently told Frans.

Oh, what a recording this would be: Iris' moaning and, perhaps, her horny shouts. Oh, how much his lover, Hans, would enjoy this!

Still Frans was a bit tense that evening. Just imagine she would find out ..., then there would be the devil to pay! Iris was by nature alert and subconsciously she was on the alert after she had found that a naked picture of her had disappeared from their 'bedroom collection' she watched over like a hawk. She had not confronted Frans with it, but was 'subconsciously' extra alert, like after a burglary.

Instinctively Frans was aware of this and realized that the slightest error could be fatal. The Dictaphone, Olympus, lay on the bottom shelf of the nightstand on his side. For safety he had already switched it on while Iris was in the bathroom. "Are you coming, darling," he called out impatiently. He was both in a hurry and not in a hurry. In a hurry because of the Dictaphone that was running, not in a rush because he wanted to drag the foreplay as long as possible to boost her horniness during intercourse to the stage of hysteria.

Iris abandoned herself to the kisses on her neck, shoulders, arms, back, legs and breasts. Frans loved to keep kissing her until she started moaning softly, for only then he was sure he had brought that part of her flesh to life and only then his mouth would move further. But tonight out of pure calculation.

Iris closed her eyes and felt the electricity build up, spreading, now shooting away from her moist toe to her erect nipples. Oh, that delicious rising voltage in which twinges of pleasure sped like thunderbolts through her, oh, so sensitive flesh, just as new and fresh as in the beginning of their love affair. Yes, Frans loved Iris, *romantic love,* but he also loved her brother, *sexual love,* the indirect influence of GSA: shadow GSA.

Frans was by nature morally decent, but in this area - fulfilling Hans' desires with regard to his sister - he was totally immoral. "*L'immoraliste*", in the words of André Gide, the famous French author.

The microcassette recorder was running silently, so Frans thought. Iris, blessed with an acute sense of hearing, suddenly asked, "What's that buzz?"

Frans jumped out of his skin. Alarm makes you inventive. "Oh, the alarm radio, the sound button is still on, just noise."

Iris didn't have the least suspicion and sank back into her rose cloud. Frans, on top of her, had started telling and fantasying about Hans and Anna. Instantly he felt the effect: the rhythmic pulsing of her vagina, and while he raised the tempo, thrusting faster and harder, fantasying ever more evocatively, he felt her vaginal contractions gradually grow stronger like the rhythms of de Falla's Fire dance. Near the climax Frans exclaimed, "I'm Hans, he is fucking you, do you love it, darling?" The atmosphere was fleetingly spoilt, as she put her finger against his lips. A bridge too far …

A bit later: "I'm Hans, you're Anna," Frans panted. "Say, fuck me, fuck me Hans, I want only you!" Completely in sexual trance, totally disinhibited, her prefrontal cortex poor in oxygen, Iris repeated, shouting hysterically, "O. Hans, fuck me, fuck me, darling. I want you, only you!" GSA temporarily escaped from its cage! At that instant Frans and Iris came. A fantastic orgasm , after which Hans collapsed like a burst balloon. At that very moment a bleep sounded. Frans filled with horror realized the microcassette was full, the alarm signal for the secretary. "What is that?" Iris asked in surprise, suddenly fully awake. This time, too, Frans reacted adequately. As he turned around to switch off the cassette recorder with one hand and twiddled with the radio knob with the other until the voice of the BBC broadcaster filled the room, he said, as casually as possible, "Oh, the radio alarm was still on, how stupid."

Iris was too dazed to react. Under different circumstances she would never have been duped. Oh, once again a narrow escape …

Erasing the tape and leaving only her final words and her moaning was a piece of cake. Oh, what a fantastic catch! How excited Hans would be. This would be the tangible proof for Hans that it was true what Frans had always alleged: that in bed they always fantasied about him and Iris and that she was madly in love with her randy little brother in these bedroom fantasies. *Bullshit!* A gross lie, but this was concrete proof wasn't it? Fabricated, manipulated, but Hans would lap it up and his passion and sexual desire for Iris would be raised to unprecedented intensity. That excited Frans more than anything …

Frans was not aware that he was playing a very dangerous game. By giving Hans the totally false impression that Iris consciously lusted after him (in the bedroom) he might possibly have the frankness to approach his sister in a most objectionable manner. With all its dire consequences …

Frans was in love with Hans, sexually in love, as Hans called it. In fact Frans was - at least in bed - also potentially 'romantically' in love with Hans, but Hans didn't allow such 'sentimental things', kept him emotionally at arm's length.

Inwardly Frans often struggled with the mystery of his passion for Hans, since he actually had, like most 'normal guys', a physical horror of men. He couldn't figure it out, sometimes day-dreaming it might be because Hans looked like the male counterpart of Iris or perhaps Hans had been his wife in a previous incarnation.

Of course **shadow-GSA** remained for Frans as shadowy as ever …

Fast forward

Only when many years later Frans had sought the help of a psychiatrist (see epilogue) he got an answer that satisfied him intellectually and reassured him a bit.

"Look at it this way, Frans," the psychiatrist explained," Just like Iris and Hans you are also - albeit indirectly - a victim of GSA, genetic sexual attraction. It is a matter of algebra, so to speak.

Given A, B and C, or in this case F (Frans), I (Iris) and H (Hans). In terms of GSA the following holds:

As mathematics tells us: If $A=B$ and $C=A$, than $C=B$. In the same way in GSA context: $I=H$, $F=I$, ergo, $F=H$. In words: *Iris is attracted to* Hans, *Frans is attracted to*

Iris. So, according to the logic of maths: *Frans is attracted to Hans.*

All via the mysterious magnetic field of GSA. In your case the shadow-GSA."

Intellectually this explanation - so logical - was for Frans an enormous relief. It was again proven: he was no homo, but a 'mono', because of GSA influences.

****

A week later Frans and Hans met in a motel, Motel Amsterdam, along highway A9. The first thing Hans eagerly demanded as they were sitting on the sofa, "You got the tape?" Frans nodded, took the Dictaphone out of his pocket and switched it on.

It was the first time ever that Hans heard the moaning, the randy shouts and noisy orgasm of the woman he secretly adored, his own sister. The recording fulfilled his most ardent wish. Oh, if Iris knew about this! Frans saw Hans' cheeks glow with excitement, his pants rising like a tent. He put his hand on Hans' fly, massaging gently, while Hans played the cassette over and over again. Hans was in a flush of pleasure. The impossible - to hear Iris' horniness - had become reality. *That she lusts after him in their love-play. What a revelation!*

Of course Hans had no idea that the reality was a bit different. Frans had said during their love-play, "I'm Hans, you're Anna." In her disinhibition she *was* Anna fucking Hans. In her disinhibition GSA had fleetingly escaped from its cage and her erotic yearnings for Hans had been given free rein. Frans' deception was a matter of nuance; the main message was true: Iris lusted after her little brother, but that she would never admit, not even to herself.

Frans had also made a Polaroid picture of Iris when she was in a daze of ultimate horniness.

From the foot, while Iris showed her pussy. In the picture you saw her breasts and face only in perspective. Central was her pubic area with those incredibly swollen labia: as large as a circle segment of a thick small pancake (cut a pancake into three portions, then the two outer portions are circle segments). Before and after, Frans, despite his many girlfriends, had never seen anything like that: flapjacks!

How could Frans have taken this picture while Iris didn't trust him one bit in this regard? By using a trick. Supposedly because the first picture went wrong (he had quickly hidden it). All pictures Frans made in the bedroom were locked up in the safe, of which only Iris knew the combination, as she suspected Frans to show them to his girlfriend(s), who all fancied Iris. Under the pretext of, "I lust after your naked pictures when we make love," Frans had managed to show Hans some exciting pictures of Iris. But this one with the enormously swollen labia while Iris was super randy was by far the most exciting for Hans. He couldn't stop looking, while Frans opened his fly and spoiled his dick. Frans lifted his head and asked rhetorically, "You fancy Iris cunt?"

"Oh, her divine, big, juicy cunt," Hans panted in a muffled voice.

Frans kept kissing him till Hans cried out, "O, darling, you're driving me crazy." That was the sign that Hans was close to coming. Frans wanted to postpone it as long as possible for this was just foreplay, wasn't it?

Frans got up, removed his clothes and jumped in bed. Hans followed suit. Usually Hans was passive, like a woman, and allowed Frans to do his thing (ass-fucking had never occurred to Frans). Frans could do as he pleased, except kissing him on the mouth, Frans' dearest wish.

Hans lay on top of Frans and started kissing him passionately. Frans feels his long, muscular tongue with coarse papilla's - so totally different from a woman's - rubbing against his palate, and imagines himself in paradise. He feels perfectly happy, a feeling of bliss more intense than he had ever experienced in bed before. Hans' nose presses against his and Frans looks at Iris' face, not a woman's face but a boy's face, in his eyes a stunningly beautiful youth without a trace of effeminacy, despite the fact that Hans sometimes, when they were necking, would say such silly things as, "You make me completely feminine," or, "You emasculate me, dearest," a word Hans had made up on the spot.

Now, lying on top, Hans was the 'man' later, lying below, the 'woman', passive and feeling feminine, without being effeminate. Frans was amazed and delighted that Hans kissed him, something he'd never done before and allowed Frans when he lay on top to kiss his full, red, sensual mouth.

Before, Frans was only allowed to kiss his nipple, which made Hans once remark, "A pity it is not sensitive."

It was for both, but especially for Frans an unforgettable night, full of lust and almost romantic love, intensified by their fantasies about Hans and Iris and by being aware of the 'perversity' of their homo-erotic love (bed love). On parting Hans asked if he could have the photo. Frans shook his head and said, "No, too risky. I'll bring it along each time." So, bait.

When Frans started the engine he marvelled over the fantastic evening, especially the kissing and as he left the parking he wondered dreamily whether Hans had been so willing out of super horniness from the tape and the picture, or because Hans had kept his word about the 'REWARD' if Frans delivered the goods. The only stain on the evening was that Hans put his finger on his lips each time Frans, in Hans' words, was about to say 'sentimental things'. But one time in a rose cocoon he did it all the same that evening. It went like this.

Frans lay on top and looked besotted at Hans who lay dreamily with closed eyes below him. In a daze of total love Frans said softly, "Oh, my Adonis, how beautiful you are," and almost in a whisper, "I love you, I love you." He wasn't looking at a MAN, not even at a boy, but at the masculine version of Iris, a totally different being altogether.

Hans opened his eye with a loving gaze, breathing, "But that can't be, that can't be ..."

Frans kissed Hans passionately and their tongues curled around each other as wet bodies of a pair of lovers.

It was the most romantic bed moment ever in their long relationship.

Three milestones

11

Introductory remark by the author

As an amateur novelist but professional psychotherapist (psychiatrist) I can't resist the urge to insert a brief chapter in which a number of factors that have pierced Iris' armour of common decency are discussed. Her suit of armour was reinforced by her Catholic faith and the idea that her deceased biological mother could observe everything from the beyond.

While in her brother, Hans, GSA and testosterone were given free rein, the situation was totally different with Iris.

In the interplay of forces between GSA on the one hand and sense of values on the other, the latter had the upper hand by far.

Without Frans' unremitting manipulations Hans would not have had a snowball's chance in hell.

The very high threshold the conspirators would have to overcome to stand any chance at all, was however somewhat lowered in the course of time (years) by a number of psychologically meaningful experiences of which I mention for a better understanding just three.

Catholic faith, Bible and incest: the British Museum

Just as the inquisitive Catholic boy who masturbates wants to know the Church's position with regard to this 'sin', so Iris was intrigued by the question concerning the position of the Church on incest, under cover of the, oh, so sinful behaviour of her sister, Anna (partially self-deceit due to the underground influence of GSA, the erotic attraction Hans exerted on her).

Her 'Aha'-moment came when Iris - who studied Latin and Greek in high school - [such an institution is called in Holland 'gymnasium' and entrance is by strict selection only] one day, while staying at one of her English aunt's in Yorkshire, visited the auxiliary branch of the British Library in the small town Boston Spa to consult a number of Latin texts, among which *De Civitas Dei* (The City of God) of Augustine, who, with Thomas Aquinas, is the most important philosopher of the Catholic Church.

She was curious what Augustine had to say about the incest question. St.-Augustine explained that incest (between brother and sister) was accepted and necessary in the new-formed world ('compellente necessitate'), but as soon as the population of the earth had sufficiently grown it became a requirement to spread the net of 'social affection' ('socialis dilectio') wider by marrying outside the family. Incest was not an interdiction by God (the Bible is full of incest; even Abrahams' wife, Sarah, was his half-sister, Iris had read somewhere), but had to be curbed by man. This required laws, human laws, to enforce the 'taboo'. Moreover Augustine had much confidence in the natural aversion of man to incest (humanae veracundiae quiddam naturale et laubile = a natural and admirable human shame).

Involuntarily Iris thought of Anna, her sister, who knew no shame and of Sacha, her sister-in - law, who told her once that she had had intercourse with her older brother from her tenth until her fourteenth birthday without any shame and without any sense that it was wrong.

Iris was curious what the other authority, Thomas Aquinas, had to say about this tricky problem. With approval confirming Augustine's view that in the beginning (after Adam and Eve) incest was necessary for population increase, etc., he added the following argument to declare incest taboo, "To live together within the family leads inevitably to sensual lusts and offers irresistible opportunities and so the incest interdiction is necessary."

He stated, "Natural affection for a member of the family can easily become flaming physical lust." *That's certainly true of Hans,* she thought, as her flesh got a bit moist.

Aquinas reported with assent, Iris read to her amazement, that Aristotle in his work 'De animalibus' tells the story of a stallion who had covered his mother unbeknown to him and when he discovered what he had done jumped from a rock in horror.

Iris almost jumped from her chair and couldn't suppress a hysterical fit of laughter, to the great annoyance of those present in the stately reading room.

Her uncle bred horses and she knew that covering a stallion with his mother or daughters was a favourite strategy. But she wanted to consult Aristotle's work. "Yes, indeed," the grey-haired librarian said, "but only in Greek."

"No problem," Iris smiled, whereupon the woman almost lost her lorgnette. Indeed, this fantasy was mentioned, but somewhere else in the treatise Aristotle discussed in full the finding that stallions cover their mothers and daughters.

In good spirits and somewhat relieved Iris left the building. One thing she had learned: the pastor had been talking nonsense. Incest was, according to the two greatest authorities of the Catholic Church, not a 'natural sin', like murder. Incest taboo was not a divine interdiction, but a human construct of the Church to restrict the love between brother and sister that can so easily degenerate into physical desire.

So incest is not inherently 'evil', just socially undesirable since the earth is now sufficiently populated. *What a discovery, what a relief!*

Not that this had any influence on Iris' instinctive revulsion against incest, but unconsciously this had made her armour a few millimetres thinner: the thickness of that of the average non-religious woman.

The second factor that had made the heavy armour psychologically a bit thinner although Iris had, of course, no notion of it, was a Belgian movie about incest between brother and sister Frans and Iris had seen on a rainy afternoon. It was such a romantic story, so refined and psychologically subtle, with two beautiful young people, who, unwittingly, step by step, were driven into each other's arms, that Frans and Iris, left the movie theatre deeply moved and in silence. Frans - unscrupulous - wondered, 'Would this be a positive message for Iris?'

Yes, in its 'existential' sense, no in its 'practical' sense.

But perhaps for Frans a small step in the right direction.

The third factor worth mentioning was the fact that Thea, their neighbour in their apartment complex and

Iris' best friend, married to Johan and still childless, had a three year younger brother, Ton, she adored and was secretly a bit in love with. Thea was a loose type, just like Johan, her husband. They regularly visited swingers clubs in Amsterdam where everything goes and Johan - a real macho, no homo at all - would give men a blow job in full abandon. This was before the Aids epidemic. He once told this to Frans and Iris, holding up his thumb and forefinger in a gesture of 'finger licking delicious'.

Ton, Thea's brother, a professional racing driver who owned a Porsche 911 was a good-looking guy, a womanizer who had them coming and going, except Thea, who resisted. One evening the four of them - Iris, Thea, Frans and Johan - were playing poker in Johan's apartment when they heard the unmistakable drone of a Porsche. Minutes later Ton entered the room like a whirlwind, brimming over with energy, a real Porsche driver, jolly and roguish, a personality bigger than life.

In less than no time the atmosphere was different, almost festive, especially when he handed around hash cigarettes as he inhaled comfortably. All, except Iris, accepted.

Thea and her brother danced on the hypnotic rhythm of an Argentine tango, Thea with half-closed glassy eyes, while she passively allowed their only physical contact during the stylistic steps - the *echo, giro, saccada,* etc. - to be Ton's protruding fly sticking like a short umbilical cord against Thea's belly.

Iris, completely sober, looked on in fascination and wondered how her friend could change from one moment to the next into a slut.

It became a lot worse. Johan opened Ton's fly as he lay on the carpet and started to blow him. Everybody, except Iris, thought it was the most natural thing to do.

"Thea, give me a hand," Johan lisped, half-drugged, while he pulled her from the couch as she almost fell on top of him. A bit later Johan and Thea licked with outstretched tongues at Ton's glans, while Ton with his hands in his neck was enjoying the blow job with a blissful expression on his rugged features.

When Johan invited Frans to join in Frans shook his head, despite the marihuana daze. *Not my cup of tea, only Hans,* he thought dimly.

For Iris, although shocked by the spectacle, this experience had been psycho-analytically speaking, a shining example: fellatio with your own brother was not as awful as she had always thought. Even her dearest friend did it. But her conscious thought was, "*Oh, how awful!*"

These were three of several 'milestones' on the long and thorny path of Iris gradual sliding from the high mountain of common decency, factors which made Iris' armour more vulnerable to the poisonous slings and arrows of the conspirators, Frans and Hans. But without her being aware of it ...

The cake

12

Hans stayed occasionally with Frans and Iris during the weekend for maths lessons in connection with his upcoming final exams.

Johan and Thea had dropped by for the traditional poker evening on Saturday: ante 10 guilders ($ 4)

Thea, naughty girl, had brought cakes containing cannabis. Only weeks later she confessed it to Thea.

In no time the atmosphere was different. Everybody felt unusually relaxed. Frans, who, despite his excellent English, often had difficulty grasping the lyrics now felt every word from the CD crystal-clear piercing his mind, one of hash remarkable effects.

Frans lay on the floor with Thea, her ear against his chest, listening to the slow, dull sounding strong heartbeat, another hash effect.

Iris, hypersensitive to all substances, from coffee to alcohol and now to cannabis, felt light and gay and filled with a kind of love for the whole world, like with ecstasy. Iris, basically a bit childlike and very impressionable, suffered the full impact of hash: regression in thought, feeling and behaviour to childhood. She started to giggle, speak and behave like a toddler and when she had to go to the loo Thea had to go along, pull her briefs down and help her like a mother her little daughter, all the time giggling and talking gibberish.

Back in the living room, Thea, who fancied Frans, opened his fly and started blowing him. Iris looked on with interest, without a trace of anger or jealousy: the magical action of cannabis. Thea, raising herself a bit, told Iris to do the same with her husband, Johan. Like clay in her hands she obeyed while Thea opened Johan's fly and pulled his by now hard peter out of his pants. As a little lamb Iris obeyed Thea's order to give Johan a blow job.

Without anyone being aware of it the door opened and Hans, back from a meal with a friend, stood in the room amidst writhing bodies lying on the floor, staring at his prudish sister blowing Johan. He couldn't believe his eyes.

"Would you like one of these delicious cakes, Hans? "Thea asked, while she pushed a saucer in front of him.

"Yes, lovely,"

A bit later Hans, too, lay, hash-relaxed, perfectly contented, on the floor, his head under the coffee table. Thea opened Hans' pants and pulled his still limp peter out of his fly, showing it demonstratively to Iris and ordering her to suck his cock. Meek as a little girl Iris obeyed. In her flush it seems the most natural thing to do. She took her brother's still limp penis in her mouth and slowly felt her mouth fill up with something that was getting bigger and harder all the time. At that moment she had no notion that she held her brother's penis in her mouth.

Then she started - without Thea's encouragement - all the while giggling and snorting with laughter, as a toddler sucking a lolly, to coddle her brother, leading him to paradise, ever further, ever higher, till he ejaculated in spasms of heavenly bliss into his sister's mouth, while the sticky white stuff mixed with saliva trickled down her shapely lips onto the new appropriately celestial-blue Chinese carpet, their greatest pride.

Hans was over the moon. He'd never come so gloriously. Yes, Frans' gullet was fine, much nicer than Sacha's pussy, he once told Frans, closing his fly. But this …, Iris' tongue, this was paradise.

*

The next day when Iris woke up from her hash flush she was filled with deep shame and remorse. She couldn't face her brother. What had she done, for heavens' sake? Blowing her own brother, unasked for, and in public to boot. What had gotten into her, for Christ's sake? She could tear her hair! Of course she knew nothing about the culprit: Thea the poisoner. But it had never occurred to Thea, of course, that Hans might be there that evening. A disaster: naughty Thea had not only been very mischievous; what she had done was evil through and through and irreparable, as later developments bear witness to.

**

The next day was very strange. Iris, by nature always cheerful and in good spirits, was very quiet, shy and withdrawn, with a damp gleaming haze of meekness and shame over her grey-green eyes.

Frans understood: she felt deeply ashamed towards him and herself about what had happened last evening. She blowing her own brother, *en public* to boot. How could she have done it, she kept asking herself in despair.

The question turned around in her head as a stuck gramophone record. She had never felt more ashamed and humiliated and hardly dared to look at Frans.

She knew Frans was over the moon. His dream come true. She knew from his bed fantasies and his nagging that he wanted nothing better than that: sex with Hans. And now it had happened, what she never wanted, the unthinkable. Oh, what a humiliation, what shame.

When Frans came home late in the afternoon with a beautiful bouquet of dark red roses Iris felt even more distraught than at breakfast.

Frans was in doubt: should he tell her that it was not her fault, but because of the cannabis? As 'conspirator' he'd better not tell her and Thea would probably never confess that she'd put hash in the cakes.

By keeping her in ignorance the threshold would be much lowered by what happened and so … Visions of delicious incest scenes loomed up in his mind.

On the other hand he loved Iris deeply and could hardly look at her state of desperation. Would he tell her anyway? Empathy, the daughter of love, won out in the end. Frans told her everything about the hash cake.

Unbeknownst to Frans he had made the right choice. Had he kept mum this experience would not have lowered the threshold, but would, on the contrary, have greatly increased it.

Because of the shame and profound humiliation she would (psychologically) offer even far stronger resistance against the manipulations of the conspirators. Initially Iris couldn't believe it. But eventually Iris allowed herself to be convinced and Frans noticed how her face brightened up in the course of their talk and she even dared to look at him again.

She was completely won over when Frans observed, "Remember the last time we were at Thea's and everybody was smoking a joint, except you. You refused to blow Johan when Thea asked. Yesterday when you did have hash in your body you obeyed Thea like a little girl when she told you to blow Johan and Hans. Isn't that sufficient proof, darling?"

Yes, that was evidence. Oh, she felt so relieved. Oh, she could throw her arms around his neck out of gratitude.

That night they had great sex, but Frans was a bit disappointed when Iris answered his question while in sexual flush, "Did you enjoy giving Hans a blow job?"

"No, I felt nothing, I was just giggling all the time and I almost had to puke when he came."

In the weeks that followed Iris had nearly every night a wet dream in which she kissed Hans' 'divine gorgeous cock' (that's how it felt in her dreams) and he satisfied her orally, both lying naked in 69 position in a luscious meadow and a brown cow with enormous eyes staring at them. Every night the same cow, the same scene.

Inwardly she was very much ashamed about these dreams; she even didn't dare to mention it in her diary, despite the fact that she knew Frans would never read it and her diary was moreover safely tucked away in her safe.

For the conspirators the experience had all the same produced a point scored.

In the deepest recesses of her unconscious, manifesting itself only in her dreams over which she had no control, this experience - blowing her own brother, albeit in half-dazed condition - had considerably strengthened the GSA-driven subconscious desire of her flesh.

Thanks to Frans explanation Iris realized that it was all beyond her control and that she had no reason to feel ashamed towards Frans or herself.

But shame towards Hans was something else altogether. For the time being she didn't dare to face him, didn't want to see him, despite Frans' promise he would tell Hans the fact of the matter.

But Hans had to stay with them next weekend because of the math lessons.

Iris decided to flee her home and stay with a friend. The moment she told Frans she felt regret. Just for an instant she had seen the gleam in his eyes. Since the night she had caught Frans performing fellatio in the 'boys room', Iris didn't trust Frans an inch where Hans was concerned.

In the course of time her vigilance had gradually weakened until, in her naivety, she ultimately convinced herself 'that there was nothing going on any more between those two.'

The gleam in his eye was as a flickering warning signal. But what could she do? Not for all the tea in China would she face Hans. So leave those two alone? She couldn't bear thinking what would happen behind her back. The next moment she rejected the idea.

The following weekend

13

Introduction

The second half of the eighties. Hans was now 18, adult, but just like all four brothers, the type that after forty would still remain more of a 'boy' than a 'mature man': so a 'boyish type'. He wore the rounded hair dress of the seventies, with layered hair to give it a smooth and gleaming texture and a long curved pony falling sideways. He was so exceptionally handsome (pretty, beautiful) that words like 'beauty' and 'Adonis' involuntarily popped up in people's minds when they saw him for the first time. No wonder that he, like his sister Iris, could moonlight as a much sought-after photographic model within the radius Paris, London and Dusseldorf, with Brussels as his stand. Just like Iris however never for the *famous brands,* but still …

Frans had once bought an expensive scarf at Dior in the Avenue de Montaigne in Paris. He was helped by a youth with wavy golden hair of almost supernatural beauty. *Unbelievable, never seen anything like that, and still not effeminate.*

Involuntarily Hans' image popped up in his mind: Hans, also a beauty but three classes lower than this archangel. Although Hans was hugely popular with girls and could pick the prettiest girls. He showed little interest and later married a Malayan woman, small, slight and ugly rather than pretty. For homo's, with whom he was very popular, Hans had an instinctive physical aversion, despite his homo-erotic relation with Frans. Hormonally, Hans was strongly *androgyn*: full of both testosterone and oestrogen, the female hormone.

Perhaps this high production of oestrogen, compensated by a high production of testosterone, was responsible for his sex-appeal for both women, homo's and Frans. His ultra-soft skin (like a woman's), his hairless chest, non-pigmented penis and hidden desire (with Frans) to be feminine, were just as many manifestations of the abnormally high oestrogen factor. His dream had been to become a pilot. But Hans failed the rigorous physical. So, he opted for IT-specialist, the profession of the future.

Home alone

The consequences of Thea's rash act were not minor. Not only Iris was deeply affected by it but Hans too. Especially the first week, before Frans, after an unforgettable night disillusioned him out of caution.

Hans, convinced that there was no stopping him now, was sitting on a rose cloud in the slow train from Amsterdam to Delft, full of anticipation of delicious sex with his adored sister. When Frans told him that Iris was staying with a friend he was deeply disappointed, somewhat to Frans' disillusionment. Frans was wise enough not to reveal her real motive in order to keep Hans under the illusion that Iris fancied him. Keeping mum could only serve to push Hans' horniness to new heights this weekend. Frans muttered something about her friend being ill.

What was the nature of the relationship between Frans and Hans, apart from sex? As Frans later told one of his girlfriends when she asked this question: "Standing we're brothers-in-law, seated we're friends and lying down we're lovers."

Saturday night: for both it was a night from '*Thousand-and-one-night'*, the unexpurgated edition. A detailed description would far exceed the self-imposed limits of this erotic novel. Let it be sufficient to report that it ended in a sleepless night, in which both lovers came about every hour - six times - ejaculating in the throat and elsewhere. The latter requires some clarification. While Frans and Hans, after a delicious Chinese meal, were hurriedly undressing on opposite sides of the marriage bed and were facing each other with hard, throbbing cocks, Frans heard Hans ask, "Come to me?"

Surprised Frans said, "But I'm with you."

"No, in my arse."

Frans couldn't believe his ears. *He seemed homo, yet he was not.* Frans knew Hans was no homo. Frans asked, "Do you have a homosexual disposition, love?" Hans' answer surprised and gladdened him.

"You make me homo, darling. You make me feel feminine, you completely emasculate me" (Hans invented that term). Hans candidness moved him. Frans wanted to kiss him. This time Hans didn't resists. Frans surprised him with ardent French kisses and caresses. Then, without exchanging a word Hans kneeled beside the bed.

"This will never work," Frans lisped. "First, a jelly." When Frans stuck his finger in Hans arse he felt an unusually tight constriction deep inside, the second sphincter, and thought, 'I'll never get through.' His finger remained spotless. Frans had condoms lying somewhere. Indeed, it didn't work. At that crucial moment Frans' erection wasn't strong enough to overcome the sphincter's resistance.

When Frans walked to the bathroom to wash, he suddenly felt Hans standing against him and wordlessly thrusting his condom covered penis into his arse. The fuck lasted less than a minute.

Frans felt nothing, certainly no pleasure, only the thrusting of Hans peter and a bit later the orgasm, as Hans belly pounded spasmodically against his buttocks. They didn't exchange a word. For both a weird and wonderful experience, the one and only time (before and afterwards) in their homo-erotic friendship of many years standing.

Instead of diminishing Hans' libido, it seemed as if this act had only intensified his longing for physical love that night.

If a spark is present between two people, sex leads to sexual infatuation, infatuation to feelings of tenderness and love, in short to intimacy and bonding that sometimes can be of a lasting nature. That is what was forged on that unforgettable night in the flames of their unbridled passion: an indissoluble bond of mutual sexual infatuation and desire. A real threat to the purity of the relationships with their female partners.

But who, what, was the creator of this bond, of this titanium love ring? The love nest? No, Thea, de gorgeous sorceress with her poisoned cup.

Although neither Hans nor Frans were aware of it, the baptism of fire of that night had greatly and permanently intensified Hans' sexual love for Frans, although Hans - like a shy woman - would never admit it.

A couple of days later Thea, Iris neighbour and best friend, and Iris, sitting in an outdoor café, had a cosy chat over a glass of wine when Thea said with a meaning look, "You must have spoiled Hans quite a bit last Saturday, didn't you? It was Hans wasn't it we heard moaning all night?"

White-faced, Iris felt like fainting ...

*

When they went to the bus stop next day, both men walked with a limp and felt stabs of dull pain in the groin and balls, just like Holland's greatest sexologist Dr. Theodorus van der Velde had described some 60 years earlier in his standard work, with regard to men who had ejaculated six times or more in a single night.

A final note: the second disappointment - apart from Iris' absence - Hans had to deal with that weekend was the bitter truth that Iris had given him a blow job under the pernicious influence of cannabis, not out of lust or craving. In his own hash-flush Hans had not noticed the difference that evening. Frans *had* to tell him to prevent Hans from doing anything rash, with disastrous consequences for their ambitions.

Pictures

14

It was Frans' fondest dream to show Iris a picture of Hans and Anna, his sister, in bed together. That would give a tremendous boost to the credibility of his stories and 'bed-fantasies'. Thus far the only evidence Iris had was that she had on one occasion seen Hans come out of the 'girls room' and a bit later, Anna, both with a guilty and drowsy look. Convincing, *but more is better,* Frans figured.

Hans' half-hearted attempts - on Frans' suggestion - to take some secret pictures during their love-making had come to naught. Anna was too observant and careful.

One day Frans had a brilliant idea.

Anna always wore exotic rings of synthetic in all colours of the rainbow no one else was wearing. Why not take a picture with an exposure lever with Hans naked in bed and a hand holding his peter.

A hand with one of Anna's exotic rings. The hand of a prostitute. Hans thought it a brilliant idea. He immediately saw the two-fold advantage of such a picture. Iris would be totally convinced and so would get turned on even more by Frans' stories - which excited Hans - and Iris could look at his nakedness without embarrassment, for after all the picture was all about the depravity of her sister, not about his penis.

The result turned out to be a great success, objectively registered by Frans' seismograph, this time his forefinger. By first telling a story about Hans and Anna without the picture and a few days later with the picture he was able to establish the effect objectively. The quakes in the deeper layers of Iris' mount of Venus *with* the picture were much stronger than without. The picture showed a woman's hand with a gaudy green plastic ring touching Hans' hard penis as he was lying on his back looking at the camera with a timid smile .The surroundings revealed only the white sheet and the pillows. Yes, Iris now knew for sure that it was all true and of course Anna didn't want to be in that picture. But that silly ring, *that gave her away.*

That little detail must have slipped her mind.

**

There was still another picture of Hans' genitals that would exert a profound influence on Iris' (suppressed) erotic receptivity towards Hans.

Here is the story.

The 'breakthrough' was the phimosis operation to correct the narrow foreskin that caused Hans more and more trouble (pain) during erection. After keeping putting off, Hans had finally decided to have it done.

The operation took place in a small clinic near the Vondelpark (Amsterdam's Hyde Park) where he had to stay for a few days to recover. The pretty young nurses fought to tend to him and were all smitten with that hunk, so cute and *that* to boot. Just as in the case of a cosmetic operation pictures were taken before the operation, immediately after and 6 weeks after. Later the pictures and negatives came into possession of the patient: standard procedure.

The moment Hans looked at the pictures he immediately understood their enormous significance in their unremitting battle against the bulwark of Iris's moral rectitude. Even he himself saw the difference: his peter both limp and during erection was far sexier than before the operation. Hans almost felt like Narcissus, pleased as he was with the result. And no more painful erections!

Now something about the pictures themselves, all full-sized and of course in colour.

To produce an erection most clinics make use of the standard method used in sperm tests: the patient masturbates, with or without porno pictures. This clinic made use of a more advanced technique: the erection pump. This was originally developed for impotent men and works via the production of a vacuum in a plastic cylinder holding the penis. At maximal vacuum (below the pain limit) the erection (amount of blood) is about 20 percent greater than can be achieved even at a young age. With the aid of an elastic ring around the base of the penis the erection can be maintained for some 30 minutes. Younger men of course don't need this ring.

Hans' pushed the pictures taken directly 'after' aside. He shivered with disgust. What a bloody mess. The pictures taken six weeks later almost send Hans into raptures, as he realized that the sex-appeal of his pecker had greatly increased for women with a fine eye for male beauty, like Iris, as Frans had told him.

Before, his glans during erection was like a veiled face, with only the forehead showing. And the mucosa of his glans! With narcissism - thinking of Iris - he stared at it, mesmerized. Blood red and vulnerable as the inside of lips, instead of coarse and scaly like chapped lips as the glans of most men from the rubbing against the underpants.

Every disadvantage has its advantage. Since his glans had always been protected by his long narrow foreskin, it had remained in 'pristine' condition. Now he was reaping the harvest, in the faint hope that Iris too would pick the forbidden fruit: a hybridization between a large, ripe banana and a juicy red plum, the resurrection of his masculinity.

Frans showed the pictures of 'before' and 'after' to Iris during their love-making under the guise of a medical curiosity (which she bought in silence). Iris showed little emotion. But his seismograph registered a magnitude 3 on the Richter scale, while colourless magma from deep below Mons Veneris seeped upwards, staining the snow-white surface.

Her perception was Iris' greatest secret, *Oh, how exciting, what male beauty and so huge!* (The result of the erection pump: 20 percent larger than normal). *And his glans: for the first time completely uncovered and, oh, as delicate and vulnerable-looking as a kid's. Oh, what a huge, little darling, no wonder all the nurses were crazy about Hans.*

Unarticulated these thoughts whizzed through her mind.

All of a sudden she realized - again unarticulated - that she was in love with his peter because it was Hans' peter. That realization threw her into confusion. *Was she in love with her own brother? Oh, if only he were her nephew …*

Outwardly, looking at the photos, she seemed placid enough. Inwardly, Iris was in turmoil. She definitely didn't want to show how much these pictures turned her on. Out of shame and the knowledge that it would be grist to his mill.

Home alone

15

When Iris, because of Thea's casual remark, learned that her husband and Hans had been fooling around all night she had been upset for days. The worst thing was that she couldn't talk about it with anyone and she was not the type to confront Frans. She had to deal with it in silence. In her bottomless naivety it did not occur to her for a moment that this was only the top of the iceberg. On the contrary, she thought it had all been her own fault: leading them into temptation by leaving. After all, when the cat is away the mice will play. Just as when she caught Frans red-handed in the 'boys room' blowing Hans, no penny dropped. Ignorance brought peace of mind and after a few weeks the trauma had largely dissipated, leaving only deep traces in the dark recesses of her subconscious.

Without being aware of it, the combination of fellatio with her own brother, albeit 'under influence', and the sight of the juicy 'medical' pictures of Hans' genitals constituted an intoxicating cocktail, a love-elixir, for her oh so sinful flesh.

Months after the cannabis weekend the following event took place, a milestone in the push of the conspirators.

Although Iris was ashamed to face Hans she couldn't keep on hiding her head. This time Hans would come on Thursday instead of in the weekend, stay the night and leave early in the morning.

He arrived at 5 p.m. Iris didn't feel particularly tense because she knew that Frans would be home at around six. A bit later he called to tell her he had to work overtime and wouldn't be home before ten. It was a lie: a conspiracy. A conspiracy born out of a remark Iris had made some six months ago when Hans might be arriving early in the afternoon and so she would be alone with him for some time. She had protested that she didn't want to be alone with him since she sensed he had designs on her, perhaps might even bother her. Frans had said, "You don't have to be afraid, darling he won't rape you. If you don't want anything to happen nothing will."

Her answer had surprised him greatly. With flaming eyes she had protested, "That's mean of you to shove it all on me. I'm not made of wood."

Oh, how Iris, without realizing it, had given herself away.

This conspiracy was the direct outcome of her unthinking remark, "I'm not made of wood."

Frans had told Hans to be 'more aggressive'. Hans obsession for Iris, almost morbid by normal standards, was fed by GSA, a phenomenon totally unknown in those days.

Frans had made it very clear. If he (Hans) wanted to 'capture' her (that is, have sex, like with Anna), then there was only one option: to seduce her sexually. The normal approach, the 'soft' way, with flowers, professions of love, touching, kissing, etc. was out of the question. "So," Frans said with impeccable logic, "you have little choice. I know you feel inhibited in her presence. But if you want to seize the opportunity there is only one option: to surprise her by showing your cock, preferably with an erection, of course. You have nothing to lose and perhaps something to gain." Frans told Hans about her remark, "I'm not made of wood." That gave Hans courage.

For the rest, despite this excellent piece of advice, Frans had no idea how Iris would react. Women are inscrutable; what excites a man could be counterproductive in a woman like Iris. Maybe she would get browned off with Hans. They had a meal at seven. So, without Frans. Hans always helped with the washing-up (at the time they couldn't afford a dishwasher). This time Iris felt his hard cock occasionally pushing gently against her behind as he put a dish back, as if accidentally. Iris pretended not to notice and found it - as she much later told her psychiatrist - rather piquant. She didn't feel threatened at all. Hans was very sweet and the place breathed an atmosphere of intimacy, a bit sultry but not threatening. Very different from when Frans would have been present.

Suddenly Hans (Frans' idea) pulled a little box from his trousers pocket and asked, acting mysteriously, "Do you want to see something girls are not supposed to see?"

Iris stopped washing and said defiantly, "Now, show me."

He dropped the box, opened his fly with lightning speed and out jumped his cock, like a stallion from his stable.

Iris, immobile, gave a suppressed cry, her hand against her mouth, as she stared mesmerized at his enormous hard-on rhythmically swishing against his open fly.

Later Iris answered her psychiatrist's question, saying, "Yes, of course I was shocked. Terribly, but I was also fascinated. Because of this I now understood why Anna would have reacted the way she did, pulling away his French textbook, as Hans was masturbating."

It gave her a fright, but she was not scared. She knew Hans wouldn't hurt her. Executing Frans' instructions he asked, "Will you touch me?"(IT, of course).

Expressly Frans had warned him not to ask, "Will you kiss it?" Hans wanted to push her hand against his peter but she resisted, so he only managed to push the back of her hand against his throbbing dark-red glans.

Frans had told him to jack himself off right away. You can excite every woman - even your own sister - to the core by ejaculating in front of her, was his theory.

With very quick movements Hans brought his organ in record time to an explosion. Iris, numb like a rabbit in the headlights, kept staring, her eyes wide open, as the white stuff gushed jerkily out of his pulsing glans. The semen spurted against her apron, the kitchen floor became slippery. No word was spoken. Hans walked out of the kitchen, leaving Iris in a state. Who had to clean up the mess? Iris, of course. While she was on her knees scrubbing the floor Hans stood in the doorway and said in a hoarse voice, "I think you're a beautiful woman. Look." And he pulled his white, flaccid but still swollen penis out of his pants right in front of her raised red face.

Minutes later Hans was gone.

*

Weeks later in bed when Frans had made her super horny with his tales she had answered his question, "Were you randy?" by confessing, "I don't know, but

I know that if he had persisted at that stage I couldn't have resisted."

"What you mean, you would have screwed Hans?"

"No, of course not, but perhaps I would have touched him or something."

"You mean you would have sucked his cock?"

She blushed in the dark and gave no answer.

The electric heater

16

Frans loved Iris, but just as a father loves his daughter but still abuses her, so Frans - unscrupulous in this regard - considered Iris also as a sex object and prey for his male lover's insatiable erotic hunger.

It was in the middle of winter. Iris' sisters had all left the parental home and Frans and Iris slept in the 'girls room' when they were spending a weekend in Amsterdam. The boys too, except Hans, were now living on their own.

The 'girls room' had always been unheated, but recently the room was heated by a parabolic electric heater that, by focussed radiation, made the bed comfortably warm. The only drawback was the soft rosy glow it produced, which however didn't prove to be annoying.

While before they slept naked under a warm blanket after making love, now the bed was nice and warm like a tanning parlour and usually Iris, after great sex, fell asleep on her back, wearing a blissful smile, naked, uncovered, in the soft glow of the miracle heater, with Frans in extended foetal position at her side.

Frans had paid it out of his own pocket and had ordered it from the US. **PrestoHeatDish-Parabolic Electric Heater.**

The brochure began with:

* *Focuses heat where it is needed most ... on you.*
* *Keep you toasty warm so there is no need to heat the entire room.*

The soft rosy glow gave Frans a fiendish idea: to give Iris a sleeping pill and then let Hans behold his beautiful sister lying completely naked and perhaps even finger her. *Oh, what an exciting thought!*

*

Finally the big day arrived. Frans had given Iris a sleeping pill under the guise of a vitamin pill.

When Frans, listening to her audible quiet breathing knew she was in a deep sleep, he cautiously got out of bed to fetch Hans. Iris lay on her back, like always after sex. Frans thought, *what good luck for Hans and how beautiful she is, just like a girl from a Renoir painting, svelte and yet voluptuous, a delight to behold with her young ripening beauty, full breasts and rose nipples to kiss, to eat, like a peach.*

How Hans will stand and stare in silent enjoyment the first time he would see his adored sister stark naked.

The mere thought excited Frans enormously. When Frans entered Hans' room he was sitting naked on the edge of his bed with a hard-on in the rose glow of the night lamp. They didn't exchange a word. Frans nodded and together they walked on their toes to the landing. The bedroom door was open.

Hans stood in the doorway and looked at his sister. What must have gone through his mind as he saw his beautiful sister stark naked for the first time, his sister he was secretly madly in love with (GSA), literally the woman of his (wet) dreams, also while masturbating.

The only thing that betrayed his emotions was his peter. At first it stood erect under a 30 degree angle, now it was standing pressed against his belly. How much Hans must have enjoyed it; oh, what a stroke of good luck to have a lover who sacrificed his own wife on the altar of his lust.

Iris gave - so it appeared - a deep sigh and moved restlessly. In slight panic Hans shot away to the safety of the landing.

Frans nodded that everything was OK. Gingerly, Hans enters the room again. Both anxiously watch her breathing.

Hans stands near the edge of the bed and they already had fantasied about all the things he would do with his sister in her state of stupor. His glans against her nipple and if she became restless dart off to the landing. Frans gives him a signal, pointing to his peter and her nipple. Hans doesn't stir, looks at Frans anxiously, afraid she might wake up. Frans stands next to him, pushes him against the bed, grabs his peter and moves it toward her nipple. Still too short. Frans gives a sign that he should bend over. Obediently he follows Frans' instruction, one hand leaning on the head of the surrounds of the bed. *Oh, what a terrifically exciting moment: Hans dark-red pulsing glans pressing against Iris' nipple.* Very gently. It lasts only seconds. Her breathing remains quiet; deep end regular. Hans had told Frans what he wanted most: kissing her nipple and smelling her pussy. Hans had already smelt Iris 'cunt mucus on Frans 'penis' some time ago in the cellar of the 'parental home' after Frans fucking Iris just for this purpose. Hans had been so randy that he licked it from Frans' penis, to his lover's delight. But this was even better: the real McCoy!

To smell her cunt and savour the heavy randy smell of her fresh cunt mucus with his nose buried in her pubic hair! Since both are convinced the drug had been effective they venture far more than when she had been just asleep. This is a delusion because the sleeping pill, a benzo-diazepam with an unfamiliar name was no stronger than the sedative Valium. But that Frans didn't know.

Frans signals with a gesture that he may kiss Iris' nipple. Hans hesitates as she is moving slightly; her breath stops short for an instant, at least so it appears. As doctors at the bed of a comatose patient they watch her, all ears. Then all is quiet again. Nothing the matter. Frans pushes Hans a bit aside, bends over and takes her rose nipple gingerly between his lips, while Hans looks on with his ears pricked up.

Now it is Hans turn. Frans nods encouragingly. Hans bends over, his left arm leaning on the wooden head. Frans stands at the foot to have a better view. Hans takes his sister's nipple between his lips and Frans notes that he is very much on his guard, afraid she might wake up any moment. He glances at Frans, askance, while he holds her nipple between his lips without sucking. Frans nods encouragingly, makes a gesture to continue.

Hans' hard-on swishes against his belly, for Frans an overwhelming sight. In his lewdness Hans loses all caution and starts greedily sucking her nipple. She is half-unconscious, he thinks, wrongly.

Frans is a bit uneasy. Not so hard, he wants to warn him but he gives no sign. What a sight, almost a mystical experience! Suddenly she moans softly. They are scared out of their wits and dart off to the landing where Frans can't resist sucking Hans' hard-on as Hans warily looks around the corner.

No, nothing the matter, she is still fast asleep - half unconscious - they think. At their planning they had not even seriously considered the possibility that Hans would get a chance to smell or lick his sister's cunt, since, like most people, she would eventually roll on her side. But now she's lying - *what a stroke of good luck* - on her back, legs spread out. Frans makes a gesture towards Iris' pubic area. Hans understands, kneels and bends over her belly. Frans pushes him aside: too weak from that distance. Frans pushes his nose into her luxurious pubic hair and smells. Hans takes his place and nods in agreement, yes, now he smells it clearly: heavy, oh, what a randy smell. Different. Hans' face is reddish and a bit swollen from excitement. Frans watches from the foot. Oh, how gorgeous she is! Renoir-rosy and voluptuous in the rose aura of the electric heater. *The sleeping beauty.*

More was not possible, she closes her legs, her vulva now cruelly hidden from view and hungry tongues. Spreading her legs would be too risky. Frans gives a meaning look at the doorway.

The show is over.

*

In Hans' bed the afterglow of the momentous experience continues. "Did you enjoy smelling your sister's randy cunt?" Hans only reaction is, "Will you kiss me, darling?" Below, that is. In that state of ultimate pleasure it was for Frans the most natural thing in the world to assume the 69-position and push his hard against Hans' face. Hans almost never gave Frans a blow job; he was like a woman who enjoys cunnilingus, but rarely indulges her partner orally. Without Frans having to insist Hans takes his cock in his mouth.

While Frans and Hans 'deep-throat' fuck each other, their bodies writhing in abandon, the door opens. Iris, in her dressing gown, stands in the doorway. Bewildered, in a daze, both lovers raise their flushed faces, letting the cock slip out of their mouth.

The door is slammed shut and only Iris' subdued spasmodic sobbing disturbs the silence of the winter night.

St-Moritz

17

"The darkest hour is just before the dawn."

Iris liked homosexual men. She thought they were rather sweet. She knew a lot of gay men from the world of fashion, but she found the homosexual carry-on instinctively 'disgusting', especially in married men, like her own husband. And with her own brother to boot; almost as awful as her husband having an affair with her sister, or even worse.

After this latest incident, too, there followed weeks of icy silence. Fortunately, she would go to St. Moritz with her best friend, Thea. Skiing and 'after-ski': romance perhaps. They knew their husbands wouldn't mind, and goaded by Thea, a slutty type, Iris had 'learned' that getting off with a ski-teacher was the pinnacle of feminine success. But this time would be different. Already on day 2 they met two cute Englishmen - real hunks - on the slopes, who had invited them for a drink in the elegant bar of Badrutt's Palace Hotel.

They had gone to the hairdresser and spent more than two hours dolling themselves up. The girls were all set for a wonderful night. They were ready at ten and sitting on their stools at 10.30. They had arranged to meet at 10.30. At half past 12 they were still sitting all by themselves, disillusioned and frustrated, nipping at their fifth cocktail. What a let-down!

> Thea, like most men and women who knew her, was secretly 'in love' with Iris. Iris made a hit with everyone. Thea was 'bisexual', just as, potentially, most women for that matter, which had been shown in 'sociological field studies.'
>
> In an article in TIME magazine in the seventies when group sex in motels was popular in the US, a scientific field study of a participating anthropologist (sociologist) showed that whereas only 3 percent of the men (all from married couples from the suburbs, doctors, lawyers, etc.) performed fellatio 'in-between', nine out of ten women (90 percent) indulged in lesbian love-making 'on the side'. This shows that, unlike men, the vast majority of women are 'potentially' lesbian, i.e. bi-sexual.

At one o'clock they went back to their hotel room. Ten minutes later they were in bed, a double bed they shared to hold down expenses. That night they were sick and tired of men, all men. What do women do when they are disillusioned with men? They seek comfort in each other arms, as the famous French writer Colette sensitively describes in her autobiographical novel *Claudine*.

The next day Thea wrote in her diary about her lesbian conquest.

It began like this:

I felt Iris' mouth close to mine. I could have easily kissed her. I was madly excited. Immediately I was conscious of the frustration of my desire. Should I kiss her? I knew Iris had no interest in women. I knew she would humiliate me. The moment passed. Then a small miracle happened. Iris put her thigh between my legs. Inadvertently, I think. I was all afire, took her in my arms and kissed her passionately, lisping in madness, "Oh, I haven't kissed a woman for such a long time." Gradually Iris' dismay, her passive physical resistance slackened. That night was the sweetest and most romantic experience of my life.

This experience had released delicious feelings and sensations whose existence Iris had never suspected. For Frans and their relationship this had the enormously liberating advantage that Iris now would be a bit less 'negative' about her husband's 'scandalous behaviour', making love with a boy, her brother, *nota bene*. Didn't she herself indulge in homosexual love? These thoughts - unarticulated - ran deep in her subconscious, but still it was balm to the wounds of their relationship.

One step forward, two steps backward

18

Our *chronique scandaleuse* approaches its grand finale, the moment the conspirators succeed by using a fiendish trick in coaxing Iris into fucking her own brother.

But prior to this a number of events took place that either advanced or inhibited the success of the push of the conspirators. Their only ally was the magnetic attraction of GSA, a silent force, unfortunately subservient to the discipline of Iris' pre-frontal lobe, seat of control, propriety and sense of values.

Three experiences are presented point by point.

- Although at the time Frans and Iris still lived in an apartment in Delft they had the disposal of an attic, as their flat was on the highest floor. There, Frans had a space made into a bar and an adjacent dim-lit room for dancing cheek to cheek, or even closer. At one of these intimate parties Hans and one of his brothers, Frits, had also been invited.

    Iris couldn't hold her liquor, in the sense that after her third glass she would become overly sweet and willing towards men she rather fancied. Like her brother, Hans. When she was dancing with Hans that evening in the 'dark room' in a manner deemed too intimate between brother and sister, Hans saw his golden opportunity: to kiss her on the mouth. That night she wrote in her secret diary: *It was such a weird and wonderful experience. It was like kissing myself... Never happened before. I was totally upset and confused.*

[Author's comment: a typical GSA effect, often reported, see Wikipedia]

- One night when Frans and Iris had been married for over a year and Hans was staying with them for the math lessons, Frans got an idea that bordered on madness.

  The following night while having sex with Iris Frans got out of bed to fetch Hans in the adjacent guest room. Hans was sitting naked on the edge of the bed with an enormous erection, waiting. Everything - their bedroom, the small hall – was in dim darkness. Frans, supposedly gone to the toilet, which he flushed, lay down again at Iris' side.

A bit later Hans enters the bedroom with a hard. He stands near the bed. In the dim light from the lampposts around the large square only silhouettes can be detected. Hans, who thought Iris would be asleep when Frans would come and fetch him, bends over and whispers, rather loud, in Frans' ear, "She is awake." Frans is greedily looking at Hans' clearly visible pale throbbing cock very close to his face. Seconds later, Iris, hysterical, darts out of the bedroom, shouting, "Perverts! You two just stay together, dirty homo's!" Frans is more than delighted at the thought of spending the whole night entwined with his male lover. Minutes later Iris storms back into the room, chasing Hans out of their bedroom like Jesus the money-changers out of the Temple.

The weeks that followed were strange and unreal. But time heals all wounds, also those of filth and marital treason. Certainly in a couple like Frans and Iris, who know they are inextricably bound to one another whatever happens. Much later Iris reproached Frans for not having protected her.

What does she mean? Did he have to beat Hans up? He, the instigator?

All Frans could do was remain silent. *If only she knew ...*
Yes, he had been literally out of his mind on that fateful night. Mad and totally irrational. Any sensible person would have known that this could only end in a fiasco. What did he achieve? *Niente,* only one step backwards, perhaps ten steps. The third 'point' requires a separate chapter.

The plaster

19

The crazy, almost criminal idea was born in Frans' feverish brain from the following experience.

Frans was running, besides his work at the University - like 'many' technical people - a small alternative practice, this one specializing in bio-resonance therapy (no matter). It employed only one assistant, Tineke, who was doing most of the actual work, operating a high-tech medical machine made by Siemens. The place, which contained a studio couch, also served as a love nest for sex with his girlfriends. Iris and Frans had a rather 'open marriage' and sleeping around (within limits, course) was tolerated on both sides, although Iris would rather remain uninformed.

His latest conquest was Bea, a spontaneous, cheerful divorced woman with a great sense of humour, with whom Frans had great sex at her home or in his 'practice'. He even had once stuck his ear in her cunt in a state of ultimate pleasure.

He dreamed of a trio with Hans and Bea, but 'knew' instinctively that Bea would reject this proposal out of hand. Bea knew all the stories about trio's with Hans and knew they had a sexual relationship. Frans had given Hans a key to the premises and one evening as he was making love to Bea she heard the front door gently being opened ... "Who is that?" Bea asked in a bit of a fright. "Hans." Minutes later Hans (whom she'd never met before) stood naked in the doorway with a hard-on.

For Bea it turned out to be an unforgettable night of ultimate pleasure. No one before had indulged her so wonderfully as Hans, the magician of cunnilingus (by the way, he never fucked Frans' girlfriends, although Frans didn't mind a bit, but only performed cunnilingus).

Frans' attention was exclusively focussed on Hans' peter, while Hans was doing his thing.

The lesson Frans drew from this experience was: *Treat them rough and tell them nothing.* Confront them with a *fait accompli.*

If Bea would have known Hans would be coming she would have pulled out. Frans knew the type. So Iris, too, should be taken by surprise, by a '*fait accompli*'.

He believed ('knew' from his 'seismograph') that Iris deep inside fancied her brother enough to make this strategy a winner.

Yes, Frans was sure of it. The IDIOT ...

**

Frans and Hans had planned the matter weeks in advance. Hans came almost every weekend for maths lessons for his finals. Weeks before the planned event Frans went during sex to the toilet in the hall under the pretext that he had been drinking too much coffee.

It had been Frans' idea: to install black plastic curtains in the bedroom, claiming the dim light from outside bothered him. The room was now pitch-dark at night.

Since the traumatic experience when Hans stood naked in their bedroom the bedroom was always securely locked when Hans was staying.

During the preparation phase (weeks) Frans had asked Iris, as they were lying in 69-position, to grasp his buttocks, claiming this would excite him even more.

In reality the plan was that, after Frans had supposedly gone to the toilet and Hans slipping right behind him into the bedroom, had assumed the 69-position. Iris would feel on Hans behind the same plaster Frans had put on his bottom days ago, allegedly because of a pustule. Then the slightest suspicion that she was sucking her brother's cock instead of her husband's would be instantly squashed.

She would of course find out when it was too late, when she had swallowed her brother's semen. Frans had talked himself into believing that he could claim for his defence that after all Hans' 'medical pictures' and his stories about Hans and Anna always turned her on. Moreover, she had already performed fellatio on her brother, albeit under the influence of hash and that she had enjoyed it too, hadn't she?

He would be able to argue, "Subconsciously, suppressed, you wanted to experience it at least once, like Anna. This, darling, was the only possibility to give you that ultimate experience."

Men are from Mars, women from Venus. Frans understood really nothing about the female psyche. But the strongest - and most stupid - motivation for this plot was his experience with Bea. She had, mind you, never even met Hans before and yet became super horny. So, *treat them rough and tell them nothing. For their own good. Women don't know what is best for them, what makes them randy as hell.*

The night in question - it was about ten o'clock - Iris was in the kitchen cleaning up. Between the kitchen and the small dining space was a connection via the bathroom with douche and washbasin, which could of course be closed by two doors. The door between bathroom and kitchen was closed and Iris knew Hans was brushing his teeth. While Hans stood at the washbowl Frans was on his knees sucking Hans' hard. All Iris had to do was open de door to surprise them! As always Hans, once aroused, wanted to come, but Frans stopped short. He wanted Hans to stay super randy and preserve all his semen for the big event.

As agreed Hans would be waiting naked until he heard Frans in the hall. When Frans would enter the bedroom Hans would slip in right behind him.

While they were lying in 69-position Frans said, "Sorry, darling but I have to pee again." Frans raised his head from her pubic area, turned the key and walked into the hall. A bit later, after having flushed the toilet, he slipped back, feeling Hans' throbbing glans against his bottom. Frans knew Iris lay waiting for the reassuring click. Yes, she heard the click. She felt safe. Iris lay in pitch-dark, longing for Frans' cock. She was on her back, naked, her labia swollen with pleasure. Frans had deliberately brought her three times close to orgasm to drive her crazy with lust.

Frans had instructed Hans, since he knew how ardently he would perform cunnilingus on Frans' girlfriends, that he should kiss her cunt gently and tenderly, as he himself always did. "It is also in your own interest," he had added superfluously, "then it lasts a lot longer before she comes, so you can enjoy it much longer, also her sucking your cock."

Frans knew Hans would get very excited when he smelled the heavy sexy, unique perfume of Iris' cunt since - as mentioned earlier - Hans had smelled it a few times before on Frans' penis. Hans had never smelled such a wonderful heavy, intoxicating cunt smell, he had told Frans. That's correct. As to this, Iris' intoxicating randy scent is as unique as her enormously swollen labia when she is super randy.

Yes, Iris had heard the click and felt safe. *Oh, if only she knew her brother was again standing naked in her bedroom ready for action!*

Iris knew Frans was fooling around with Hans and always kept a sharp eye on those two, leaving them alone as little as possible. Frans sensed it. But occasionally she had to stay away longer, as at the hairdresser's. On one such occasion Frans had rehearsed with Hans. Frans in Iris role, lay on his back, fully dressed, just in case ...

The main thing was to show Hans how he, Frans, after an alleged pee, resumed the 69-position in the dark. First kiss her pussy and then slowly with his right leg over her head, assume the correct position. Then, lower his belly until he felt her lips around his glans. As a hungry little bird her mouth would then bite into his cock, he had assured Hans. Frans had also instructed Hans to shave closely as he had a much heavier beard than Frans.

*

But back to the present. Yes, Iris had heard the click and knew it was safe. Not that she was afraid Hans would ever try again, but the click offered certainty; it was just the idea.

How did Frans feel? Was he horny? No, the overwhelming feeling was regret. Suddenly the enormity of what was about to happen hit him in its full scope.

And this time he could not profess innocence. Now Iris would know he was the mastermind behind this outrage.

Frans heard Iris moan softly with lust. It was a sign that Hans was licking the cunt of his beautiful sister.

"Oh, how wonderfully big you are," Frans heard her mumble with a full mouth. Then Frans knew Iris had the sexy huge cock of her own brother in her mouth, enjoying it, savouring it, 'knowing' it was her husband's. Iris moaned again, louder this time, despite the neighbours and her brother in the adjacent guest room. Again she cried with a full mouth, "Oh, you're so wonderfully big tonight, darling," With her arms clasped around Hans' buttocks, Iris 'subconsciously' felt the plaster: the double insurance against the least suspicion.

While the waves of unprecedented carnal pleasure washed over her flesh (*Hans was the cunnilingus magician*) and her brother's thrusting penis made her almost choke as her mouth overflowed with semen, she realized in a flash from Hans' muffled moan that it was not her husband but her brother lying on top of her. An unspeakable feeling of helplessness, like falling into a deep well, overwhelmed her, but as long as the spasms continued she was totally helpless, entirely at the mercy of the glorious orgasm that seemed never ending.

An account of what happened next can be left out. Two years ago when Hans stood naked in the bedroom the atmosphere had been cold and weird for months. Now a Siberian winter had descended on their marriage, which lasted for almost a year, turning into a bleak spring. Would their marriage survive this trauma, this criminal rape?

Let what follows be told twice, from a slightly different perspective.

Like in someone fighting his own addiction, the experience, aided and abetted by the blind forces of GSA, had strengthened rather than weakened her carnal receptivity to the fatal attraction of her little brother. In a sense the conspirators had both lost and won this round.

But on a human level: what had Frans achieved? A brief moment of ultimate pleasure. Their marriage was disrupted. Frans had completely lost her trust. Only in the deepest layers of her flesh, brain and psyche the gloriousness of her orgasm and the '*fellatio on the gorgeous cock of her own brother*' (she had seen it near her face as she switched on the table lamp in a state of panic) had left deep traces and activated the dormant forces of GSA.

Would GSA ever be transformed into SEX, like MAGMA into LAVA?

The darkest hour is just before the dawn.

Thanks to the diagnosis of Frans' sterility and Iris' ardent desire to have children, undreamed new possibilities arose, the subject of the next chapter.

The condom

20

A year after the plaster-incident the wound appeared to have healed. In a basically good marriage it seems as if the digestion of a terrible event runs its course like the mourning period after the loss of a beloved: after a year the worst is over, the mental pain diminished or gone.

As Frans and Iris had by now been married for several years and since Iris still hadn't become pregnant, they decided to visit a fertility clinic. It turned out that Frans was the problem. The result of the sperm test: normal number of spermatocytes, but a too low fructose content. End of the story.

Iris intensely longed for motherhood. IVF was still in its infancy, adoption seemed a hard and tortuous path. A sperm donor looked like the best solution. But in those days sperm donors from sperm banks were anonymous, rather scary. But - *mirabele dictu* (wondrous to relate) - there was a potential sperm donor in their circle of friends. Frits Tuinman, a colleague of Frans and friend appeared willing to act as a donor. The natural way, of course.

Frits found Iris of course a piece and Iris was rather charmed by him, who, incidentally, was a devout Roman Catholic.

After three attempts over two menstrual cycles Frits decided to quit as he could not endure the idea of having a child with another woman. So, adoption appeared the only option. A discussion with his friend, Roel, gynaecologist (he has been mentioned before) gave Frans a highly original 'theoretical' idea.

When Frans told him the result: a too low fructose content, Roel said, "Hmm, interesting. The current view is that fructose, or, really, fructose-acetate is the energy source (fuel) for the spermatocytes on their long, difficult journey to the Fallopian tubes where the egg is implanted. A layman might think, 'Why not just add a bit of fructose', but it is not that simple. Experimentally it had been shown, both in humans and in test animals, that only adding an ultra-filtrate of semen (so, without the spermatocytes) is able to make semen with a low fructose content fertile. But this requires a rather complex procedure. In the first place …"

Frans had stopped listening. He got an idea, perhaps a brilliant idea, so it seemed to him. Why not ask my brother Albert to give a helping hand, or rather his eleventh finger. With the aid of a porous condom with pores that filter fructose but retain the spermatocytes. Iris liked Albert and they sometimes flirted a bit innocently at family parties. Albert had a family with two kids, so he was fertile and could thus provide the fuel.

The idea was simple. Immediately after Frans had ejaculated, Albert would take his place - with the porous condom - and ejaculate in his turn.

The porous condom would ensure that the fructose and the fluid would be filtrated and Albert's spermatocytes retained. So, the child would carry Frans' and Iris' DNA. No more adoption but the real thing! The only problem was where to get a condom of the right composition.

As a boffin he didn't worry about that small detail. When Frans presented his - what he called - crazy idea as a 'theoretical' solution to Roel, Roel immediately saw its rationality. "Not a bad idea. You can, of course, always hire someone for that chore and who wouldn't want to fuck Iris. The only problem is to produce such a condom and how to find the right material."

Suddenly Roel got a brilliant idea. "I got the solution. Why not use the material they use for kidney dialysis filters. They allow small molecules like sugars to pass but retain large molecules like proteins. Well, a spermatocyte is far bigger than a protein molecule, so …"

"Bingo, "Frans cried out enthusiastically. But he saw one problem. "Condoms are made from latex or lamb's gut, dialysis filters from synthetic."

"No problem," Roel assured him, "There are also condoms made from polyisoprene or polyurethane, so, plastics. By the way, it is best to order dialysis filter material from Porex, the biggest producer. But of course you must order more than one condom. Fortunately, the stuff is very cheap."

The discussion ended with Roel's remark about Frans' sperm, which Frans had brought with him in a vial. After Roel had studied the spermatocytes under the phase-contrast microscope and counted them, he said, raising his head from the ocular, "Yes, the number of cells is normal, although your sperm is on the thin side, In your case this is because of the low fructose content. Half of the viscosity is due to the fructose content. Odd, isn't it?"

Frans, a man of boundless energy once he'd made up his mind got going right away. POREX, the producer of dialysis filters, advised the use of polyethylene, the material also used in dialysis. This came in handy as Borealis, the largest producer of condoms with a plant in Geleen (the Netherlands) also produced, beside latex condoms, polyethylene condoms.

The Director of the Boreolis subsidiary in Geleen was most kind and very cooperative after Frans had explained the problem. "No problem. I regard it as humanitarian gesture," he assured Frans, "We'll use the Porex material, but the minimal number will be one thousand. That will cost about 500 guilders." Three weeks later Frans received a parcel in his letter-box. A thousands condoms from the Borealis plant in Geleen.

Roel had told them they should be patient. They had to reckon with at least 6 sessions, two per cycle, to give it a chance. Also, the 'donor' had to remain 'inside the vagina' for some twenty minutes, because of the slow diffusion of fructose and its 'co-factors' through the pores of the condom.

"Twenty minutes!" Iris had cried out in a fright. But yes, 'a clinical necessity'.

Before asking Albert they had placed an ad in a newspaper for a 'donor'. No response. Although Albert had immediately, even with a certain eagerness, consented, it proved no success. Already after the third session Iris pulled out. She couldn't summon the courage anymore. Physically, Albert repelled her more and more. He was the very opposite of Frans: short, overweight (90 kilo's), a softy, a bit effeminate. She liked him as a brother-in-law, but this ..., and then another 20 minutes with him on top.

Moreover, so she justified her decision to herself, the future mother should feel happy and relaxed during intercourse, otherwise the child would experience its negative effects and she wouldn't want to run that risk for all the tea in China. Despite Frans' pleadings Iris remained adamant.

Only then THE IDEA occurred to him. He always tackled a problem 'analytically'. What are the options left? They couldn't find a 'donor' for hire. So, what remained? Only Albert and Hans. Theoretically, that is. Albert was out. So, only Hans. He would be over the moon and surely wouldn't mind stirring Frans' mash in his sister's cunt. The only obstacle was Iris.

He thought the odds were - given her strong maternal instincts - four to one; so, worth trying. If he played his hand right she would go along. Her craving for motherhood (with Frans genes) would be greater than her revulsion against incest. And besides, this was the last straw, wasn't it? And it was just a medical necessity, like receiving blood from a family member. Nothing to do with incest His argument would be: 'You want a child and preferably with my genes. The only one left to provide 'fuel' is Hans and we both know that he wants nothing better than to sleep with you. You had sex with Albert, whom you find unattractive. You often told me that Hans is very attractive for women, so, for you too, and you never denied it. You don't have to feel awkward towards Hans, as he knows this is purely a medical question. Hans will stay over the weekend and as soon as I come he takes over.'

"But Hans happens to be my own brother!" she had protested emotionally." If he had been my brother-in-law or my nephew it would have been a very different matter."

Eventually, after much arguing and perseverance on Frans' part, lasting days, Iris gave in, although her feelings rebelled against it. She had come to realize that this was indeed her final chance to have a child with Frans' genes, the man she loved to distraction, although he was sometimes a real bastard.

But now the greatest psychological hurdle loomed for Iris: she couldn't fuck him just like that, stark naked, could she?

"Well, then you just put out the light," Frans said. He knew she hated to have intercourse in pitch-dark. Moreover the black plastic curtains had been removed long ago and now the bedroom was always dusky at night from the lighting outside as mentioned earlier. Frans offered more suggestions.

"Why don't you two first go to a disco and kiss and cuddle in the car. Or, let's go to the sauna the three of us." Iris didn't think much of it. She admitted the real problem for her were his peter and her breasts. She loathed the idea to face her brother, bang! stark naked on that particular night. She knew she would clam up completely. Not very good for the chances of getting pregnant and for the foetus for that matter. Finally, Frans proposed they would first spend an evening naked together without touching, like on a nudist beach. Then she could get used to it. Oh, no, that would be *so* scary ... She shuddered.

Eventually he yielded to Iris' own proposal. Hans would come a couple of days earlier to spend the evening, The curtains of their living room would be drawn because of the neighbours across the huge square. Frans would be present, of course and would be 'in charge', like a referee. Hans was not allowed to undress; Iris just had to get used to looking at his peter (everything from the past had been erased from her perception) and she would expose one breast to overcome her deep sense of shame.

Frans thought it a silly idea from her point of view. He almost 'knew' she would feel much more embarrassed then just 'bang, in the nude'. Inwardly he grinned like a sitar. Perhaps it would be an interesting evening, with him as emcee.

***

Iris was very nervous but didn't show it. Frans had told her, "When Hans is helping with the washing-up and supposedly presses against you by accident to pick up a dish or something, just pretend not to notice."

"I can't imagine he would dare to do that again, "she reacted.

"No, that's right, but I'll tell him to, without telling, of course, that I discussed this with you."

Eventually Frans succeeded in persuading Iris that such an innocent physical contact would be a good preparation for the naked contact during intercourse.

The particular evening arrived. Hans came at seven and would stay for a meal. Instead of a dress Iris was wearing a sexy blouse with one bare shoulder. The meal passed off free and easy. No mention was made of the TOPIC. At the washing-up Iris felt now and again something hard against her bottom. She pretended not to notice. Frans had suggested to have a sherry.

"You don't want to ply me with liquor, do you?"

"No, of course not, darling, but it relaxes a bit."

Curtains drawn, lights dimmed, languishing background music. Hans was sitting on the couch, nursing a drink. Iris was sitting in an easy chair nearly opposite him, with Frans on the piano stool and the coffee table in the middle.

A bit ill at ease, in almost solemn tones, the Master of Ceremonies, scraping his throat, began, "Hans, I have told you everything about our problem and Iris and I are most grateful that you're willing to help making Iris' pregnant. Whether it will be successful is another matter. You know how prudish women are and this is, of course, very difficult for Iris, to have to fuck her own brother, even if it is purely for medical reasons. A blood transfusion from your own brother is not as bad as a semen infusion." He thought he was being rather funny, but no one laughed. "Standing in your trunks is OK, then Iris sees 95 percent of your nudity, but, for a woman, and definitely your sister, it is all about that one-tenth of a percent, your peter. Of course Iris has to get a bit used to that before she's ready to bed you. My proposal was that she would see you naked first, but that she refused, didn't you, darling? Too scary for her. So, the only thing left is to show Iris your prick tonight and Iris shows you her boob. Also very hard for a woman baring it to her own brother. Yea, Hans, that's the way women are, a very different breed from us, men."

Rather blunt, but how else should I have put it, Frans thought. Against the background music an awkward silence followed.

Provoking on purpose, Frans said, holding Iris' hand, "Darling, open your blouse, or shall I help you?"

"Why me first?" she reacted panicky.

Frans noticed that Iris had applied mascara to her long silken eyelashes overshadowing her grey-green eyes that inadvertently stayed focussed on Hans' genital area. She looked different: like the photo model she was, like an actress, enchanting in her flowered blouse with one bare shoulder that looked divine on her.

"Hans, open your fly and show your dick to your sister, "Frans said, deliberately rude. Maybe Hans was tense or not quite in the mood yet, but as he pulled down his zipper and bared his peter it was still limp, even without any 'swelling'. He did this without any shame as he kept looking at her. The moment he opened his fly she averted her eyes. Iris didn't dare look. But she had to.

"Love, if you don't look it's all useless, don't you see?"

Overcoming her deep sense of shame she forced herself to look and keep looking, all the while taking little sips of her sherry.

"Hans pull back your foreskin and show your gorgeous glans to your sister."

Hans obeyed, as he always obeyed Frans' instructions, and as he let go of his peter Iris and Frans saw his penis quickly grow thicker, longer and harder until the throbbing blood-filled rod reached its maximum expansion, rocking on the waves of lust.

In his excitement the Master of Ceremonies lost all sense of decorum and called out, "Darling, don't you find him gorgeous? Don't you get a sopping wet pussy? Your brother's wonderful prick coming in your cunt?" (He was referring to the following week).

Frans was horny, with a hard-on. "Iris don't you want to touch him, feel him?" (Of course, not IT, but HIM)

As if stung, she recoiled in her chair.

"Oh, no, I wouldn't dare," she cried, gesturing in protest.

Frans had promised on his word of honour: no pawing. So, this was his first transgression, at least verbally. It was now Iris' turn to bare her breasts. When Frans said as much, like a school teacher, sitting on the armrest and wanted to open the buttons of her blouse she stopped his hand, the instinctive gesture of a woman.

Frans, getting rather impatient, was very insistent. Finally she gave in. To Frans pleasant surprise she was not wearing a bra, *so, she had prepared herself in earnest for this occasion.* Frans opened her blouse completely to bare her Renoir-tinted, ripe breasts, sensual, seductive, now fully exposed to her brother's delighted gaze. Hans called out in rapture, "Iris, I knew you were beautiful, but *so* beautiful!" She blushed.

The dramatic little scene reminded Frans of the beautiful slave in the painting, *'Vente d'un esclave à Rome"* by Gérôme in the Hermitage; the way Iris covered her breast with one hand, the other covering her downcast eyes, while greedy eyes licked her nudity. Within less than a minute she wanted to close her blouse again. Frans, said, "Iris, just a bit longer, Hans, you like Iris' boobs?" "Divine," he gushed in a hoarse voice, "Oh, Iris how beautiful you are. I've always been madly in love with you. May I kiss your nipple?"

The Master of Ceremonies was adamant. "No, Hans, we agreed, no pawing."

As Frans was still sitting on Iris' armrest he said with an inviting gesture, "Just stand here for a moment, Hans, so Iris can take a close look at your gorgeous prick."

In a flash Hans was standing right in front of his sister, his beating rod level with her red half-open lips. Iris now really looked, without shame or reserve. From her shining rose cheeks and the glitter in her shrouded eyes Frans could see she was excited.

In his excitement Frans tossed the toga of Master of Ceremonies bluntly into the laundry basket.

Against all promises he started to masturbate Hans in front of Iris' dilated eyes. Suddenly he stopped, as he noticed Hans was close to coming. Hans, yet not totally without shame darted back to the couch where he frantically tried to stop the orgasm, stamping his feet, stretching and beating his legs spasmodically, doubling up, desperately shouting, "Don't come, don't come." In a panic, Frans repeated parrot-wise, "Don't come, don't come, love." Too late.

Iris saw her brother's sperm gushing jerkily out of the dark red glans, the urethra wide open like a spouting mouth. Total confusion. Both Iris' and Hans' first thought was the precious new light blue Chinese carpet, the showpiece of their living room. Fortunately the damage was minor as Iris immediately swung into action.

That same night (Hans left at 10 p.m.) Frans asked during some heavy fucking, "Do you find Hans attractive as a man?"

"I find him awfully attractive, but you can't talk me into fucking him. Thrice, three times, no more!"

Lovers

21

Iris had agreed, it would happen next week. In the meantime not a word was said about this during the day.

Frans noticed that Iris was rather tense. Only during love-making Frans mentioned the BIG EVENT.

"It is our only chance, darling. Just look upon it as a medical necessity and as to Hans, you don't have to feel ashamed at all. He doesn't do it for philanthropic reasons like Frits and Albert, for you know Hans is in love with you and for Hans this really is the tops …, to fuck you. Just be honest, darling, with whom do you prefer to go to bed, with Albert or with Hans?"

"That isn't fair. You know I abhor Albert in bed."

*

Hans would stay with them, but Iris was not in the mood to prepare a meal (too tense). They had a meal at the Chinese in Voorschoten (near the Hague). The service was unusually slow. They had been sitting there for two hours and not a word was mentioned about IT. Only talk about this, that and the other and family gossip.

It was about 10 o'clock when they got home and they were in bed at eleven, Hans, of course, in the guest room.

Iris had insisted that Hans was only allowed to enter their bedroom after Frans had ejaculated. He managed to convince her that this was 'technically' not feasible as Hans had to penetrate her right after his orgasm to supply the fuel - fructose - for Frans spermatocytes on their long journey to the egg.

"So he has to be present while we're fucking!" she had cried in alarm.

"Yes, otherwise too much time would be lost."

She was silent for a moment, then said, "Then bang against the wall when you're nearly coming."

Frans banged three times against the wall, but because Frans peter was nearly unquenchably on fire he jumped out of bed and walked into the dark hall where he almost bumped into Hans. Frans whispered, "When I'm lying on top of her I'll give a signal." Frans and Iris were silent. Frans threw back the sheet and started fucking her again. Frans knew it was safe now; his penis had cooled down and he had sprayed lidocaine on his glans to make it less sensitive. While Frans kissed Iris' nipple he fucked her with slow, deep thrusts. The room was bathed in a dim red glow. Iris glanced at the open door. What must have passed through her mind when she saw her brother enter the bedroom naked with an enormous erection?

But this time 'legitimate', 'medical'.

While they were fucking - Iris pelvis, too, was moving violently, synchronically with his - Iris kept staring, not at Hans' face, but at his member, the member of her own super horny brother. He was now standing at the head of the bed. His rod beat as a metronome against his belly, like the one time he had seen his sister naked in her deep sleep.

Iris had pushed away Frans' head and instinctively covered her naked breasts. Frans pushed her hand away saying softly, "Don't be ashamed, darling. The more horny Hans gets the better his sperm. "Frans grabbed her hand and pushed it toward Hans' penis. Her hand resisted, drew back fearfully. "Just caress it a bit, darling, as foreplay." Her resistance weakened. She allowed the back of her hand to be pushed against Hans' member. The back of her hand against his pulsing glans, oh, what a wonderful sight! Frans almost came. "Caress him, love, caress the stunning prick of your brother."

Iris was horny. GSA and sexual abuse had an open field. Her cunt muscles rhythmically compressed Frans' penis, the sign of ultimate animal lust.

While they were fucking and Hans was sitting on the edge of the bed watching, Frans, in his feverish lewdness, started sucking Hans' condom-enveloped penis, until Hans called out in alarm, "Don't, otherwise I come!" This was the second time that Iris really saw Frans blowing her brother. The first time – the night of the electric heater - she had been deeply shocked and completely upset. This time not at all. Had she been immunised by her recent lesbian experience with Thea, or by Thea's confession that she sometimes blew her brother, or was it the 'medical situation' in the 'here and now'? Even Iris herself would never have been able to answer the question, but one thing was sure: she was absolutely not shocked, found it even rather exciting, but dared not really look (the prudishness of women!).

Later, Frans himself was surprised about it. While he was fucking Iris and blowing Hans he was flooded by the most tender, loving feelings towards Iris. He had never loved her with such intensity! The magic of ultimate sexual arousal!

"Will you kiss Hans' prick, love?" Frans insisted, as he withdrew his mouth. She looked eagerly, with enormous shining eyes, at Hans' dark red glans wrapped in a condom that concealed nothing.

Just when Frans wanted to insist, knowing that Iris would have done it in her momentary '*sexual insanity*', he came.

Oh, what a glorious, violently jerking never-ending orgasm. Iris hadn't come yet. Exhausted and blissfully happy he flopped down on Iris and stayed lying like that for seconds, while Hans was sucking Iris' rose nipple.

Then, Frans stood up straight and called out in a commanding tone, "Hans, fuck your sister!"

Without putting up a struggle Iris allowed Hans to lie on top of her and letting his cellophane wrapped 'Blutwurst' slip into her vagina. Frans watched, but the holy fire of lust had been extinguished. He watched the scene like a very interested onlooker. Like watching a movie he saw that Hans started thrusting, while Iris remained passive at first. With Frans her loins were always moving. After a while there came some movement in Iris' loins and gradually the movements became stronger, until brother and sister, entwined and kissing, literally were fucking one another: Hans was fucking his sister, Iris, with violently thrusting loins, her favourite brother. Fucking with Hans was for Iris like dancing; a flowing, playful change in a rhythm that was not from him, nor from her, but from both. This she had never known before.

Frans became - at least psychologically - excited again and got a 'swelling'. In his flush he used the most filthy language. "Hans, your sister letches after you." But for

Frans the most emotion-releasing fact was not that they were fucking each other, wildly entwined, but the flush of love: the way they kissed one another with boundless passion and abandon. He with his tongue deep in her, and the way Iris, besotted, responded likewise, requiting his love in the body language of romance. Hans panted, "Oh, Iris I'm crazy about you, angel. I love only you. You're the most beautiful, the dearest woman in the world. I only want you."

Never had Frans experienced such an eruption of love. Yes, passion at countless sex parties, but not this. This was LOVE. Frans vaguely felt a pang of envy. Iris had never loved him this way. Hans' seminal discharge came suddenly. Frans noticed it: the way he jerked ever more violently against Iris and the way Iris bottom shot upwards as his seed gushed out of his dilated glans. Iris came at the same instant. Fountains of lust and love flooded the loving couple. Kissing and entwined they stayed lying on their side for another 20 minutes, his sex organ in hers, as the medical protocol implacably prescribed.

The next day Iris wrote in her diary:

I could fill these pages with all the horniness and love of yesterday. Torrents of kisses from Hans. The thrusts of his flesh in mine while I bend my body to a bow to better fuse with his. But, my God, this can't be, infatuated with your own brother. If only he were my cousin! Would I leave Frans for him?

The Accident

22

Iris got pregnant all right. But the biological father was not Frans, but Hans. How this could happen is clarified later: here the events leading to this 'accident' are chronicled.

The die was cast, there was no stopping them now. GSA and its effects, illicit sexual acts, had free play on that memorable first night. Two more sessions with the porous condom followed. These are not described in this 'çhronique scandaleuse', as it would be more of the same. Worth mentioning is however the first time Iris, pressured by Frans, had sex with her brother without a condom.

Frans' wildest fantasy was that Iris would perform fellatio on her own brother, like Anna, her sister, and Thea her best friend. Fellatio with your brother was in Frans perception even more 'perverse' than fucking and, so, more exciting. At his request his friend Roel, the gynaecologist, had given him a prescription for Estandron in order to increase Iris' libido temporarily. The official indication of this injection preparation - a combination of oestrogen and testosterone - is *endometriosis,* a uterus condition, but it is also popular with women for increasing their libido, like on vacation. A 'side-effect' was that the woman not only becomes hornier due to the testosterone, but also less inhibited, so, just like men, 'shameless', the ideal combination for Frans' wicked design.

Frans injected it in her buttock, telling her it was vitamin B12. Its action would last six weeks. He even showed her the empty (wrong) vial.

But already the same evening Frans noticed the effect when he started talking about the fucking with Hans. She turned out to be much less inhibited than normally. Estandron effect, GSA effect or super horniness at the recollection, or all three ?

"Did you love fucking Hans?"

"Terribly."

"Would you love it even better without a condom?"

Frans knew she hated condoms, but in their open marriage, she had to if she slept with other men, as she didn't want to use the pill and didn't wear a IUD.

Iris answered with a counter question. "But that's impossible, isn't it. What if I get pregnant? But it would be wonderful. You can really drive a woman crazy with your fantasies."

"Yes, darling, the naked dick of your favourite brother in your horny pussy. Wait, I'll get some pictures."

For the first time Frans showed her the pictures from his own private collection he had carefully kept hidden. Two: one close-up of Hans' erection and one in which he lay naked just before he came. Oh, the exciting randy expression of his femininely pretty masculine features.

The hospital pictures, too, after the foreskin operation, Iris devoured, as he could establish with his finger, his infallible seismograph.

"Do you like it?"

"Gorgeous," she lisped. And Frans knew that Iris was just, as he himself, in love with this peter, because it was Hans', her forbidden love, her delicious goblin. "He's yours, darling, all yours. Wouldn't it be lovely to kiss him, drive him crazy with your tongue?"

"Yes, lovely," she lisped, while she wasn't even in 'sexual trance'. The testosterone magic. They had great sex that night.

Yes, Frans had got Iris to the point that she was ready to have sex with Hans without a condom. But that required patience. It was only possible during the first three days after her period, the only safe interval.

The BIG DAY, a Saturday, arrived. They would have an Indonesian meal in Wassenaar, the 'suburb of millionaires' near the Hague.

They were driving in their second-hand Chevrolet Impala with its enormous tail fins and spacious front seat (like a couch) on which Hans was wedged in between Frans and Iris. The mood was - contrary to that historic first time - very relaxed and sultry from the start, amplified by Frans' suggestive remarks, like, "Iris thinks you're a fantastic lover, don't you, Iris." Frans had expected Iris to protest, or act demurely. She only smiled like a Mona Lisa and kept silent. Estandron?

When, after a delicious meal, they drove home Frans put his hand on Hans' forbidden zone. With his right hand he tried to unbutton his fly. "No, don't," Hans said, as he held back Frans' hand. Hans, not Iris, was being prudish.

But eventually Frans had undone the last button, grabbed in his underpants and pulled Hans' peter out of his fly.

It was still dusky. Involuntarily, Iris shot a side-long glance. at the still limp peter of her brother, his glans still fully covered by the long - but widened - foreskin.

"Iris," Frans called out excitedly, "isn't it wonderful to feel Hans' gorgeous prick in your cunt. Flesh on flesh. Without plastic. Does your pussy already long for her big brother?"

Meanwhile Hans' peter was growing fast. Iris stared mesmerized. Frans had trouble keeping his eyes on the road: one eye on the road, the other on Hans' member. Frans touched his peter and began to caress it. Like an exotic flower the dark red glans opened out of its covering, a sweet-ogling siren for Iris' amorous look.

"Iris, caress his dick, darling." But she didn't budge. Frans was in a flush, a flush of horniness, of sexual inebriety. There was no stopping him. He let it all hang out.

"Iris, kiss Hans' cock, your brother's cock. That's what you want, don't you. You lust for his lovely glans, don't you. You said you were madly in love with Hans, didn't you?" In his excitement he jumped the lights on the freeway in Wassenaar. It gave him a fright. That punctured the purple balloon of lewdness. The rest of the ride passed quietly and without incidents after Hans got his pants back in shape.

When they got home Iris first wanted a glass of sherry. So, yet a bit tense, Frans concluded. Little was said. A bit later they were in the bedroom. Iris went first. She lay on the bed naked. Frans treated her as a slave. She obeyed as a slave. Estandron?

Yes, the right combination: Estandron and lover. When a woman loves a man she's 'obedient'. Well, up to a point, the point being lowered by Estandron.

In turns Hans and Frans, naked, of course, kneeled across her breasts. She sucked eagerly at Frans' member, bur greedily at her brother's. Time and again she withdrew her mouth to enjoy the look of Hans' hard-on. Frans lay beside her and also started to suck at Hans' member. "Together, darling," he murmured. Their combined play by which their tongues touched each other, was only interrupted by Hans' 69-position, in which he set - in Hans' words - "*the divine, sexy, juicy cunt*' of his sister on fire with his passionate tongue. Iris moaned and wriggled her pelvis from pure delight. Frans, used to Iris' beauty was surprised: over and over again calling out, "Iris, how beautiful you are, how beautiful you are!" She had never been this beautiful.

The coitus of the siblings was for Frans a feast for his senses and his sensibility: the notion to watch brother and sister fucking and now without the medical necessity as an alibi, but from pure horniness and infatuation. Iris was, if possible, even more in love than the first time. She lay across the bed with her buttocks on the edge of the bed, while Hans standing with an enormous erection very slowly approached her vulva as if he wanted to tease her or perhaps wanted to offer his sister the opportunity to watch in slow motion the loving approach of his penis to her vagina. Iris looked with stretched neck, looked and looked. Frans saw she was completely in a sexual flush, on cloud nine. Again, Frans briefly felt a vague pang of jealousy. She had never been that much in love with him, not even in the beginning.

"Darling, wouldn't it be heavenly, the naked cock of your brother in your cunt?"

"Heavenly," she lisped. "Hans, darling, come in me, come in me," she moaned full of desire for his penetration. Oh, the sight of the fucking. Fantastic! Frans watched in delight; the way Hans was fucking his sister standing, thrusting deep in her, but ever so often withdrawing his white penis in order not to come too quickly. And Iris all the time looking, with stretched neck and hungry eyes.

She pulled Hans by his shoulders towards her. Then the kissing began. Oh, their passion, their moaning, and endearments. "Darling", "Angel".

Hans: "I love you, you're the most beautiful woman in the world, Iris. I want only you, love."

And Iris in her love flush, "Hans, my darling, you drive me crazy. I want you, only you," She was out of her senses, on cloud nine, reinforced by the subconscious sense of the enormous sin, the taboo, the perversity of fucking your own brother, to be madly in love with your brother. When Hans and Iris, exhausted but deeply happy lay beside one another, Frans was lying with his lips near Iris' vulva.

"Just kneel for a bit, Iris."

"Why?"

"Then Hans' semen runs out."

She did what Frans wanted. Hans' sperm, diluted by Iris' cunt's mucus, trickled slowly into Frans' greedy mouth. With his mouth full Frans kissed his wife. Greedily, like a baby bird being fed by its mother she lapped up her brother's semen. "Don't swallow it yet, darling. You must enjoy it as long as possible." She stuck her tongue deep into Frans' throat for the last drop of semen.

While they had a chat afterwards Frans had a strong feeling that he was the odd man out. Was he annoyed? Mixed feelings.

Iris wrote in her diary about the strange feelings this experience had released in her, ending with:

I dream the craziest things about Hans. The day is empty. I am imprisoned. And Hans? What does he feel? I'm taken completely by surprise. I lose everything. I stagger. I only have the sense of yearning, carnal desire, terrible longing. For my brother, the most gorgeous man – boy - in the world.

Abused

23

Although Iris felt a strong desire to make love with Hans only - she was madly in love and could only think of him (GSA?) - she had not given in to this impulse, also – strangely - because of the fact that Hans had just been married six months. To Sacha, a Dutch woman of Malay descent. Short, dark-skinned, smart, but no beauty. Everyone was surprised that such a handsome lad, who could pick up any girl, would choose to marry such an 'ugly duck'.

Meanwhile Frans and Iris had moved from their flat to a detached house in a 'nice neighbourhood' in Delft. It even had a driveway, a spacious living room, the territory of their huge Danish dog, Daniel, downstairs, and their bedroom on the first floor.

One evening, some weeks after their first '*coitus à trois*' without a condom, Iris had become so excited by Frans' stories, fantasies and their mutual recollections, that in the middle of the night Iris almost hysterically cried out, "Call Hans, let him come right away!" Frans suddenly realized that Sacha was visiting her parents in Singapore. Iris' idiotic outburst of temporary sexual delirium was not that crazy after all. He grabbed the receiver, dialled Hans' number.

"Hans, Iris longs for you. She wants you to come right away. She wants to indulge you." The last remark was a fabrication, but she was too horny to protest. Frans had told Hans that the front door was unlocked. Half an hour later they heard a car coming up the driveway. A bit later footsteps in the hall. Suddenly, Hans stood in the dimly lit bedroom. Frans and Iris were both undressed, of course. Iris lay on her back. She was super randy and 'without shame' from the testosterone, the three sherries and her extreme excitement. They had agreed on staging a kind of act to make it even more exciting.

"Hans, your randy sister wants to commit illicit sexual acts with you." He immediately understood and without a word he stood at the head. Shamelessly Iris pulled his zipper down. Frans called out, "Oh, Hans, look what your sister is doing, abusing her own little brother. Iris how smutty you are. You're worse than Anna." The words were like lashes. She was like a slave humbling herself before her master, as she was greedily sucking her brother's gorgeous cock. And then the contrast: his sister naked, he fully dressed. For a moment Frans got a fright at the thought 'unsafe'. Then he relaxed. No, it was a month later, still safe (it was in fact the fifth day after the period, not so safe, but he thought it was third day).

Hans dropped his clothes on the floor and jumped in bed, pushing Frans aside, taking possession of his sister. To make it last as long as possible Hans and Iris were lying on their side while his member hardly moved in her vagina. Iris only felt the 'rearing' of his penis and the rhythmic swelling of his glans. They kissed passionately. *Love without words.* Frans was the odd man out, but he felt no jealousy. He was enjoying the moment. Frans was lying against Iris back, his belly pressed against her buttocks. He pushed his penis under her bottom to the back of her vulva. His glans felt Hans' hard penis. He never expected it. Suddenly his member shot into the depth. He was dumbfounded. *How was it possible*! Iris labia had swollen up again to the size of thick pancake segments in her state of supreme lewdness. Was this also something like that? He didn't know that this was the result of overproduction of the hormone relaxine that the ovaries and the placenta produce during delivery to widen the cervix and the vagina, but that the ovaries also produce when the woman is in a state of hyper (sexual) excitement.

Frans in his flush only thought vaguely: *if a baby can come out , why shouldn't there not be enough space for two cocks.* Oh, the idea of fucking his wife with his lover. Frans made fucking movements, but Hans cautioned him, touching his shoulder. He understood: postponing it as long as possible like in the Kamasutra. Involuntarily Frans made imperceptible movements. Oh, what a lovely sensation. Unprecedented! Then it dawned on him that he was in fact rubbing his glans against Hans'. Not rubbing noses, but rubbing cocks, an exciting form of mutual masturbation. *Glansing,* Frans called it, rubbing cocks. But this was far better. *Glansing* in Iris' cunt while she thought she was being fucked by her two lovers. Frans and Hans started fucking each other, making use of her generous hospitality. Hans was far more focussed on her cunt than on Frans' penis. But just as Iris was close to coming Hans - bisexual with regard to Frans - made a U-turn. Frans noticed it. Iris was unaware of anything. Hans, too, was in *homo*-raptures because of the intense randy local sensations on that most sensitive spot, the back of the glans, the zone with the highest concentration of sensitive nerve-endings, the so-called lewdness-receptors. Almost on their own accord, like the notes of two violins in a double violin sonata their penises metaphorically curled around each other, as they kissed, madly in love with each other, twisting in Iris' big, but oh so tight, elastic, juicy vagina. Suddenly Hans moaned, "O darling, you're driving me crazy!"

Iris knew with feminine intuition that 'darling' referred to Frans; that Frans was not fucking *her*, but her brother in his sister's cunt. Then Frans - in his excitement – did something stupid. At that moment it was even very dumb. He bent forward over Iris' head to kiss Hans. Hans responded eagerly and with their heads above Iris' they started kissing passionately while in the depths of her flesh their rearing penises executed in an ascending ritual tempo Manuel de Phallus' *Fire Dance.*

Iris started to sob silently. Frans noticed it from the jerking of her shoulders. Suddenly she tore herself loose from her 'lovers'.

"Filthy homo's! Using me to fuck each other!" She was totally distraught. She jumped out of bed and stumbled, crying, downstairs, to the living room. Hans and Frans stayed behind, a bit upset, but the carnal lust was stronger. Later, as they were lying, satisfied and gratified, up against the pillows, Frans said, "Just have a look, Hans. Maybe you can comfort her."

What happened next requires some comment.

Under the influence of Frans' perverse mind, his fantasies and video tapes, Iris had some time ago finally yielded to the temptation: like Frans she performed fellatio on Daniel, the Danish dog, and learned to enjoy the pleasures of sexual intercourse with Daniel. It became a carnal addiction, the most exciting experience of her life. Fucking a big dog was for her sinful flesh even far more randy than fucking a man, last but not least, because of the enormous size of Daniel's bloodshot ivory coloured penis, rock-hard because of the 'penis bone' and also because Daniel was able to endlessly discharge his watery semen in large quantities into her cunt without ever losing his desire for more.

And what was safer and more hygienic than a dog's semen? No danger of infection, since canine bugs don't infect humans (apart from rabies, etc.), so no risk of AIDS and, of course, no risk of pregnancy. A better lover was not possible!

But she had stopped abruptly when Daniel, in full company, suddenly jumped on her with a full erection. Oh, the shame, the humiliation of the moment, although no-one suspected anything. After all, dogs will be dogs. They have erections all the time, even while dreaming.

Iris' clitoris was on fire, despite her anger and frustration. That, the Estandron and perhaps the 'comfort' of having intercourse in her grief, even with a dog, were perhaps the 'reasons' for her rash behaviour in the living room.

When Hans entered the living room he found Iris on the sofa, slumped, naked, her thighs spread wide, moaning with pleasure, wildly thrusting her belly, while Daniel, his forelegs extended on the sofa, was fucking her madly, breathless with lust and love licking her face with his moist, muscular tongue. She was coming. It was delicious, wonderful, interminable.

Hans stood in front of her, naked, without erection, and looked shocked at the scene, repeating to himself,

"Oh, no, I don't fancy that, I don't fancy that sort of things."

His expression of disgust and disapproval spoke volumes. Iris filled with shame and embarrassment, was unable to stop the orgasm, like you can't stop a sneezing fit. When Daniel finally withdrew his pearl-tinted cock, a large quantity of watery semen oozed out of her vagina, the result of the quick succession of a number of canine orgasms.

> If you're shocked by Iris' behaviour, the statistics are even more shocking.
>
> An anonymous American survey in 1989 revealed that one in five single female dog owners had sometimes indulged in fellatio or other sexual acts with their dog, a secret no-one talks about.

She felt more humiliated and embarrassed than ever before.
After Frans had explained to Hans that sex with a dog is 'safe' and 'hygienic' and that, besides, the dog's penis is protected by the 'sheath', Hans became milder in his condemnation of Iris' 'misconduct', which, because of his infatuation, proved no obstacle to his amorous advances. There was no stopping him now.

Signpost

24

These are the facts. The Frans-Hans duo had thrice attempted to make Iris pregnant. That had failed. In the next cycle Hans had been allowed to have intercourse with Iris without a condom on day 3 after her period.

This resulted in Iris' pregnancy.

How could it happen?

This was the result of a combination of a number of (un)fortunate factors.

Instead of day 3 after her period it was in fact day 5; a dumb error. Iris' cycle fluctuated between 25 and 30 days. This cycle was short. As always the period lasted 5 days. So, instead of the 8th day the coitus took place on the 10th day. In a 28-day cycle the fertile period is between day 11 and day 16. In a 25- day cycle from day 10. Moreover in a state of great excitement the ovulation can occur earlier than otherwise. This happened here. This is not so surprising if you recall that rabbits only ovulate during coitus.

When Frans and Iris discovered that she was pregnant, their joy and conviction were such that they left out all arithmetical work.

They were fully convinced that the final session in which Hans had been using the porous condom had been successful. So Frans was the biological father. Period.

This delusion was not exposed at the time of birth, since the delivery occurred a few weeks too early, a premature birth of a perfectly healthy baby: a girl whom they christened Ciska.

The gynaecologist' remark that this was a premature birth, with all its dire implications, had not sunk in with the deliriously happy couple.

The new-born didn't need to be put in an incubator, everything was fine!

Two years later Iris became pregnant again. Here only Frans could be the father. How could that be?

Frans, health-freak had been following a strict sectarian diet for years, with virtually no carbs (no bread, potatoes, rice, pasta), no sugar and little sweet fruit to keep his insulin level low and thus slow down aging and drastically reduce the risk of cancer. That was the diet recommended by a number of prominent scientists, among whom professor Roy Walford of UCLA. An excellent diet, but with the potential disadvantage: a too low fructose content in the semen. On the advice of his friend, Roel, the gynaecologist, Frans had abandoned this diet because of his sperm problem and injected himself twice a week with the pituitary-like preparation *pregnyl* to boost his own testosterone production, since a low testosterone might contribute to a low fructose content. Within eight months his fructose content had increased to within the normal range.

Frans hadn't told Iris about it, ensuring that the small voice of doubt about the fatherhood of her first child, Ciska, had been silenced for good. The small voice was the result of the fact that the baby was the spitting image of Iris, while she could not discover any trace of Frans' features in the girl. Biologically quite possible, but she'd had unprotected sex with Hans after all. Would she …? No, the birth of her second child, also a girl, named Ilse, silenced the whispering dark voice for good.

Frans had had serious misgivings from the beginning. When his oldest daughter, Ciska, was 14 he had removed some mucus from her cheek for a DNA test. That established beyond question that Hans was the biological father.

The fact that Frans was not Ciska's biological father merely confirmed his suspicions. Since Frans didn't want to burden Iris with this shocking revelation he kept silent.

But a lie never gets old.

Part 2

Ciska's big problem

25

Ciska, their eldest daughter, with whom Frans shared a special father-daughter bonding, had just turned eighteen. This bonding and Frans boyish nature (something between a big brother and a father, definitely not the proverbial father figure) may explain why Ciska confided her biggest sexual problem she had been struggling with for a long time to Frans when he dropped by one evening in her cosy apartment, near the Apollolaan, Amsterdam's most expensive street to live.

But there was no question of any physical or erotic intimacy. It was even unthinkable, like in all normal father-daughter relationships.

While another young woman might perhaps reveal her 'secret' to her mother, so Ciska did the same to her father without any shame or discomfort.

Ciska, the spitting image of her mother at her age, was spontaneous and stunningly beautiful, but though she had many friends (both male and female) and occasionally a boyfriend, was still unattached and had never fallen seriously in love.

Although she wore a IUD she never wanted to fuck without a condom because of AIDS, a fear reinforced by the fact that her best friend had contracted AIDS during a vacation at the Club Med when she had had a one-night stand with a nice French student.

Oh, no, never without a condom! But that was her problem. She had a strong physical need to fuck because of the abnormally strong 'sexual itching' in her vagina that could not be relieved by masturbation. Incidentally, she had told her father, she had trouble coming with masturbation or a vibrator. And only a good orgasm could temporarily – one week - suppress that 'randy itching' down there that sometimes drove her up the wall and disturbed her sleep.

The doctors at the hospital (AMC) had found three years ago that her ovaries produced too much of the weakly androgenic hormone androstenedione, the precursor of estradiol, the female hormone. This was the cause of the abnormally strong vaginal sex urge, the doctors had told her. There was no treatment.

The only thing that worked was a good fuck. But because she hated condoms - also because of the unpleasant sensation - the orgasm was 'weak' and so the 'therapy' inadequate. The 'itching' would just continue to plague her.

But since a year she had found a solution for her condition: Jacob, an old schoolmate, a nerd, with John Lennon glasses, who never looked at girls and vice versa, with whom she was on friendly terms, was her **stallion.** At her demand he fucked her once or twice a week without a condom (she knew he was to be trusted, as he was no homo either) There was only one restriction: he was not allowed to kiss her. It worked wonders. Good orgasms, no more 'itching'.

But now in a few weeks he would move to Groningen, a city some 100 miles from Amsterdam. She got sick at the very thought, she told her dad. Again that awful itching, sleepless nights.

"You think it's awful?" Frans asked rhetorically as he took a sip of the white wine. "I think it's absolutely awful, dad. I don't know which way to turn. Again that terrible itching and nothing works. Except a good fuck without a condom and I don't dare, except with Jacob."

"Oh, well, Cis, the risk of AIDS is now very small, only 200 new cases a year." Frans could argue forever, Ciska absolutely didn't want sex without a condom. And moreover all her friends were unattached and sleeping around. Oh, no, without a condom? Never!

Frans, who saw that she really had a huge problem on her hands, that she suffered terribly from this strange condition, came up with a weird but logical proposal.

"Uncle Hans works twice a year for a month in Dubai. Everyone who works there is obliged to submit a report that he is HIV-negative before being allowed into the country. Moreover he is married and doesn't sleep around. Why don't you take him as your stallion, Cis?"

"Uncle Hans? But isn't he old, bald and fat?"

"What an idea, darling. He's only 20 years older than you and he looks much younger. And he is too thin rather than too fat. You know, he's the spitting image of your mother, so, of you."

"Dad, don't be such a moron. I'm not going to bed with my uncle," she snorted disdainfully. The very idea was absurd.

But a few days later when they had another chat Frans showed some recent pictures of Hans. Cis was pleasantly surprised. Spontaneously she called out, "Oh, what a good-looking man. Yes, I always thought he was very handsome, but I haven't seen him in years. A real hunk."

Frans could see she was impressed. She had a totally different picture in her head.

Thanks to Frans' good offices her uncle (*actually her biological father*) became Ciska's new stallion. Although she found him infinitely more attractive than Jacob, he was not allowed to kiss her either: only fuck. She didn't want any emotional complications! Because of the size of his penis, his sex-appeal and sweet personality, her orgasms were even much stronger and effective than with Jacob. She was happy, relieved and grateful to Frans and didn't have the least problem with the fact that Hans was committing adultery. That was his problem, not hers.

But after less than a year it had come to an end. For his work as a IT-specialist he had to stay in Dubai for eight months. Iris was at her wits end and depressed. Back to square one. "Dad, what should I do? Again that awful itching."

The meal

Frans took Ciska for a meal in the well-known fish restaurant in the *Binnenweg* in the Hague. The topic of conversation, carried out in hushed tones, was again sex. About her vaginal problem. About her experience with Hans. Even about her lesbian feelings for a close friend - mutual, she knew - very intense, near the open fire, but neither of them had dared to take the initiative.

Here is a 'summary' of the subsequent lengthy conversation.
"Would you be seeing Hans again before he leaves for Dubai?"

"Fortunately, yes. Just one more time next week." "And the Tarzan I gave you?" Frans had bought her an expensive high-tech vibrator in the Bahnhofstrasze in Zürich: 400 Swiss francs.

"No, dad, only a good fuck works. I think it is absolutely awful that Hans will be gone for so long. I know I'll be sick to my back teeth again of the itching. Especially at night. Sometimes I won't sleep for nights."

"If I weren't your father, I would be the ideal replacement, Cis," Frans blurted out before he knew. Ciska put her knife and fork down and looked quasi-severely with big eyes at Frans and said in a dramatic tone, "Dad, your own daughter!"

"Yes, that's just what I mean," Frans hastened to say, "That's why I said, 'If I were not your father.' But anyway, and this is only a philosophical observation, look at Woody Allen, he even married his daughter."

"Don't be daft, dad. She was adopted. If you marry me you'll be clapped in jail. Now you're really talking through your hat. My own father as stallion. Now, you're really going too far, dad."

Apparently she had taken his philosophical remark as a proposal, which indeed it was. All he wanted was to help his daughter. Nothing ventured, nothing gained, he ruminated, as he took another sip of the delicious white wine and looked at her lovely face, slightly marred by a troubled expression. But his motive though weird, was honourable: he just really wanted to help his daughter in her distress.

"Cis, when I suggested Hans you were also shocked. My uncle, ridiculous. Uncle or father, just a matter of degree, isn't it?" The wine had loosened his tongue. But Ciska continued to protest, though a bit hazy from the wine her father kept refilling from the silver ice bucket. *Absurd. The very idea!*

Frans kept arguing with Woody Allen as standard bearer, that is was OK, that it was in fact the only solution to her problem. She knew her father was a health-freak who wanted to live past 100 and so wouldn't take any risks. What she didn't know was that he was a debauchee with numerous girlfriends, but that was none of her business. Moreover she had told him on a number of occasions that she found him attractive, or rather, she used to say, 'I find you and Iris a good-looking couple.'

"But the only reason that I bring this proposal up is to help you with your problem. Logically, it is the only solution."

She looked at her father sceptically, her eyes narrowed above the wineglass, elbows on the table, as they were waiting for the dessert. Then she said, "Yea, pull the other one. I think you just lust after fucking your own daughter, you dirty old man. Well, isn't that true?"

"Cis, virtue has its own reward."

She giggled mischievously. Ah, the wine! She always became very sweet, very girlish, almost docile, after her third glass. Frans saw the flush on her cheeks and the brilliance in her eyes, a bit in a flush, fanned by the wine and the topic of conversation. Frans, himself a bit in a flush, speculated, 'I wouldn't be surprised she has a moist pussy.' Oh, yea, there was life in the old dog still.

They were sitting side by side. Soft lighting. No-one in the busy place paid any attention to them. Frans was a bit excited, in a flush. He knew he was not her biological father, and perhaps that gave him some sense of freedom. Iris knew nothing. Frans grabbed her left hand and while he pressed it under the table against his fly, he whispered hoarsely, " Feel anything, Cis?"

To his great satisfaction she didn't pull her hand away as from a hot stove, but allowed it to rest passively on something hot, too. She only said, theatrically, speaking severely, "Daddy, your own daughter."

Already after her third glass of wine Ciska became a bit light-headed. Thoughts flashed as *streakers* through her mind. Her intellect whispered, 'He's right, that would be the only solution.' Her feminine sensibility shuddered at the thought. Fucking your own father!

Besides, she was eighteen, he was forty-eight. Yes, he looked much younger, thirty-five or so, very boyish. very naughty-looking. Really not at all the type of a typical FATHER. Another voice - an evil spirit? - whispered, 'Stop nagging. As a woman you abhorred Jacob. Still he was your stallion. Frans is not less attractive than Hans and moreover you're crazy about each other. It's just a matter of getting used to it, just like with uncle Hans. Besides, if it's scary just close your eyes. A prick is a prick.' Frans felt he'd made some progress, but he did realize there was still a long way to go, full of mental obstacles, and uncertainties, but at that very moment he vowed he would try everything to help her. Yes, to help, that was his primary motivation. The horniness was just a side issue, like the wake of the lifeboat. But the very thought sprouted an erection.

When they were in the car the atmosphere remained intimate, sultry, very different. Frans noticed her voice: lower, sensual. On motorway A44 past Wassenaar, Frans put his hand on her naked thigh (she always wore mini-skirts). While talking he kept it there. She didn't push his hand away and suddenly he said something really dumb, "Look, Cis, if I touch you like this (he put his hand on her genital area) it doesn't mean a thing. It just shows I really like you a lot." He noticed that she froze. Oh, how dumb, a bridge too far. But the dark cloud soon dissolved and the weather turned fine again; only the tropical sultriness had gone.

On parting at the little parking lot near her home his last words were, as she opened the door to get out, "Cis, think about it. I love you and my love will only get bigger when I take over Hans' role and you're relieved of your misery. Give me another kiss, Cis."

With her legs dangling outside she turned around and gave Frans a kiss on his cheek. Frans, hot, tried in vain to kiss her on the mouth, while his hand was under her shirt. Frans felt her cunt was moist, felt she was both randy and fearful. He gripped her chin and kissed his daughter hard on her mouth. To his delight he felt Cis' girlish tongue, soft as butter, slither in his mouth. Suddenly she freed herself from his embrace. "That's enough. You're terrible."

Frans, now fully aroused, panted, as she was standing outside, "Cis, I come with you. I want to fuck you. I want to fuck my own daughter. That must be fabulous."

Sticking her head through the window Cis said, "Dad, you're moving too fast. I've to think hard about it. That's impossible, isn't it, fucking your own father."

Frans, dazed behind the wheel, watched his daughter's silhouette dissolve in the darkness of the night.

The porno magazine

26

Three weeks later - Hans hadn't left for Dubai yet - Frans had rung at his daughter's door after making sure, peeping through the window, that she was alone. Although Ciska was outgoing, spontaneous and stunningly beautiful she still didn't have a real boyfriend, not even for a few months. All her friends were more or less going steady. Iris couldn't seriously fall in love and during the week she was mostly alone in her cosy apartment near the Amsterdam-Hilton. On weekends she would go out, paint the town red. She was crazy about dancing, the wilder the better, in psychedelic disco's, in short a partygoer, who also enjoyed a good fuck, mostly a one-night stand.

Only years later a psychologist discovered, using the Jung Word Association Test (100 words are presented and the client must spontaneously react with a word), that the cause of this inability to bond was the abnormally strong attachment to her father.

The cordiality and joy she showed as he dropped by Frans always found heart-warming. That evening was truly a father-daughter evening, no indelicate word was spoken. They chatted, played Rummicub, Frans read some poems, they played *quatre-mains*. The evening just sped by. On parting in the entrance hall long past midnight, he said, as a father, from the bottom of his heart as he took her in his arms, "I love you very much, darling."

"Me, too."

Their mutual love enveloped them like a cocoon, both closely entwined in the dim light of the ceiling lamp. He gave her a kiss on her cheek but effortless his mouth slipped to under her nose. Was it because of what happened in the car some weeks ago? Without any struggle Ciska let herself be kissed on her mouth. She kissed him back and so father and daughter remained entwined for minutes. Never before had Frans experienced his love for his daughter as deeply.

"Hey, Aapje," [her pet name, meaning little monkey] she said softly, "What am I feeling now?"

He did have an erection, not a full one, but he knew it was a '*love-swelling*' (as he called it), not sexual excitement. "A 'love-swelling' darling, because I love you so much," he breathed between kisses. She didn't know anything about such things, but she believed him. That was the way she felt: it was one of the deepest experiences in her life. Love poetry. This evening was the first step from 'rock to rock' on the slippery path to father-daughter incest to alleviate her 'itching problem' that drove her up the wall. He visited her as always, twice a week, mostly on Monday and Thursday and usually stayed no longer than an hour or so, and gradually - without mental coercion from his side - Frans approached his ultimate goal: to take over Hans' role.

There were perhaps more than ten 'stepping-stones' of psychological significance, but in this chronicle it suffices to mention the three most striking.

> But first something about what happened eleven years earlier when Ciska was seven.
>
> As was 'normal' in those days (the eighties) she would occasionally join her mother or her father in the bathtub. Ciska would sometimes play innocently with his peter, dubbed the submarine. Diving, surfacing, diving, surfacing. In the living room she loved to ride on a rocking horse: daddy's knees. On one occasion she wanted to play 'rocking horse' in the bathtub. Then something terrible happened by accident, although Ciska had not been aware of its awful significance: Frans penis had broken her hymen. At that time Frans, sly fox (predator) had subtly awakened her childish erotic imagination by transforming the 'submarine' into Bashful, one of Snowwhite's seven dwarfs. Ciska was Snowwhite. By telling bedtime stories about Snowwhite he had gotten her to the point of giving Bashful, 'who hated to be kissed', a sweet goodnight kiss. That never happened, but the erotic bonding did, facilitated by the strong natural bonding between father and daughter. Frans deeply loved his daughter, but like with Iris, he was sexually unscrupulous, using subtle seduction rather than brutality.
>
> After the failed kiss Frans never bothered 'his minor' again.

Hans had left for Dubai. As Frans had expected she started again about her 'itching problem'; tossing and turning all night. He asked her medical details about the AMC (Amsterdam Medical Centre) tests when she was fifteen. About androstenedione, the culprit.

"The gynaecologist was surprised that my hymen was absent while I never had intercourse, dad. Isn't that strange?" Frans got a bit of a fright, felt hot under his collar. Would he tell her? They were sitting on the couch watching television, she wearing a white Japanese kimono. She looked lovely and her brown areola was partly visible in the red glow of the table lamp.

"You remember the bath, Cis? The red spot. You asked, surprised, 'What's that, daddy?'. We were playing this little game in the bubble bath, riding on a rocking horse, and you felt Bashful was very big. Yea, something terrible happened then. I didn't realize it until it was too late. Because of the wild rocking - you enjoyed it, so did I - my peter suddenly slipped into your pussy. You gave a scream, remember? I thought, 'Why is she screaming?' But the red spot and the randy feeling below made me realize 'I'm fucking my own daughter.' It felt too great to stop. You enjoyed it too, didn't you? I know that, for I came in your darling little cunt-and then Bashful became sleepy and tired. I remember exactly what you said. "Don't stop, don't stop. It just such a lovely feeling."

Ciska had listened, her ears burning, her cheeks flushed deep-red. She remembered that scene vividly, almost like playing a video on a video-recorder.

"So, you deflowered me when I was seven, "she said, almost dreamily, but not accusingly. Frans couldn't have chosen a more opportune moment for this shocking revelation: the day of ovulation, the middle of the menstrual cycle. Then the woman is most susceptible, most vulnerable, the hormone level the highest. In Cis not only the estradiol production in the ovaries had peaked but also the production of androstenedione and - to a lesser extent - testosterone, the hormone largely responsible for the libido, both in men and women. That evening Ciska was as hot as a bitch in heat. The hormones were raging through her body and made her extra susceptible to his erotic advances.

Frans sensed it, like a tomcat in heat senses that pussy is in the mood. Slipping his hand in the slit of her kimono, Frans said, touching her thigh, "Yes, darling, I deflowered you, I was your very first lover. In retrospect it was really rather beautiful, wasn't it. We have already fucked. I have already come in your darling little slit. So, you never have to suffer again from that awful itch, right? Come give me a kiss, Cis, my little darling."

"Aapje [little monkey], you're terrible," she cried, as she walked to the kitchen to make another cup of Rooibos tea. While Ciska was messing about in the kitchen trying to digest the terrible revelation, Frans rummaged absentmindedly for junk in her cupboard full of papers, old magazines, cartons full of pictures, trinkets and other ornaments. All girl magazines, Girls, Viva, Cosmopolitan and much more. Ciska, just like her mother her age, was a much sought-after photo model for teens. Her pictures figured in all these magazines. Ciska was more childlike, far less mature than Iris at her age, which was also reflected in her height (1.60 m), her slender figure and small but well-formed firm breasts. Years later her psychologist told her that her mental and emotional development had lagged a bit behind because of the 'incestuous' closeness with her father, a bit like the retarded growth of children in a loveless environment. *Though here it had been just the reverse: too much erotic-tinted love.*

One day when she was seventeen and staying in London with her parents and younger sister, Ilsa, the lady at the newsstand in the Ritz even thought she was only fourteen. Her parents were not disconcerted, for sometimes Ciska, who looked younger than her age, would be rather childlike in the way she behaved, especially in the presence of her parents.

Hey, a porno magazine, there at the very bottom. Curious, Frans opened Fox Magazine, a Belgian porno magazine. All pictures of blowing women and pretty girls showing their pussy.

Ciska, his daughter with a porno magazine. Wow! At that instant Ciska appeared with two mugs of steaming hot Rooibos tea. Hastily she put the mugs on the coffee table and snatched the magazine from his hands. She'd better not done that. After a little struggle he went to the far corner of the enlarged living room and started thumbing through the pages while Ciska numbly sat on the edge of the couch with glassy eyes.

Whaaaaattt ...! Is that Cis?

Yes, it was Ciska, his daughter, naked, her thighs spread, a bit insecurely showing her pussy. Was Frans shocked? No, he was delighted!

"Oh, darling, what a cute little cunt, "he blurted out enthusiastically. Oh, the surprise to see her cunt, the cunt of his own darling daughter, the forbidden zone he had seen the last time more than ten years ago when he had emptied the bath deliberately. Then it was no more than a groove like a doll's anal cleft. Because of his reaction, totally different from what she had expected, Ciska brightened up and in a halting voice she began to tell her story.

Just like with Iris most photo shoots had taken place in Brussels. A photographer friend who had made her half-drunk, had taken her to his studio and fucked her (fortunately with a condom), taken pictures of her naked with a hidden camera and sold them to Fox magazine. "What a bastard!" Frans blurted out, inwardly very pleased. Oh, what a lucky thing that it was a Belgian porno magazine and not Playboy or another widely read porno magazine in the Netherlands. She wouldn't have known which way to turn. While he was sitting next to her on the couch he put his hand, while talking, casually on her bare thigh and little by little his fingers came closer to the middle. Her only defence was a quasi- stern "Dad, your daughter …"

His hand felt her pubic hair and stayed there. He just couldn't stop looking at her picture, the sight of his own daughter's cunt, the lovely glistening labia, like rose petals sprinkled with dew with a rosebud in the middle, her thimble-sized delicate clitoris, the result of plentiful astrodenedione. The labia of the other ladies were just as fruity and fresh, but Frans only had eyes for that one, the cunt of Ciska, his daughter and - hopefully - his future lover.

He couldn't stop kissing the photo, exclaiming, "Oh, how lovely, Cis, your darling clitoris."

"Aapje, don't be daft." But she was so relieved he reacted this way. She had expected something very different. Relief mixed with deep shame that her father saw her pussy. Not for a moment did the thought occur to her that her father might well become her next stallion. Despite the awful 'itching' and the logic of his arguments it was unthinkable.

Frans' erection couldn't escape her gaze. Frans saw her looking at his bulging fly. Impulsively, almost as a reflex, he pulled his zipper down. His peter, already escaped from his underpants, stuck his bald dark-red head inquisitively out of the window. "Look, Cis, I was allowed to see your sex, so you may see mine. Fair shares!" he said hoarsely. "Remember ten years ago when you were a bit in love with Bashful? Remember when I read to you at bedtime? I asked, will you give

Bashful a little night-kiss? Yes, you would, but Bashful was close to coming. That's why it never happened. But it is never too late, love. Do give Bashful a little kiss, will you?" He pointed at the back of his glans, just below the glans' cleft, the most sensitive spot.

She did not react with horror or fear, kept on looking, mesmerized, with burning cheeks, but said, "I'm not ready for that yet, dad." It sounded like a promise. At that moment there was a ring at the door.

Startled father and daughter sat upright, both straightening their clothes. Ciska peeped through the chink between the heavy curtains. Her mother stood on the doorstep. "Shall I open the door?" Cis asked, shaking inwardly. "Yes, do. She knows I'm here. Is better. Did you tuck away the porno magazine?"

Bubbly as always, Iris rushed into the room. The first thing she said was: "Why are the heavy curtains closed, Cis? You always leave them open, don't you?"

She asked this without a trace of suspicion, but it gave Frans a bit of a fright.

The flying carpet

27

For Frans the next few visits to Ciska (dropping by, perhaps sex) felt more like visiting a very young girlfriend he was trying to seduce than visiting his daughter. Odd. Was there hope?

Ciska's compass, too, pointed in a different direction, more to M (man) than to D (daddy). But in her case the unconscious motive was the relief of her "itching" that disturbed her sleep, sometimes drove her up the wall. Perhaps like someone with a great aversion to prednisone but still opts for it to be rid of the suffering.

Without her "itching" issue, no incest issue.

It was that simple. She paid more attention to her looks on the evenings Frans came to visit: mascara, perfume (Estée Lauder's Private Collection, his favourite scent, he once said) and could sometimes not decide which dress to wear; changing two or three times and standing for ages in front of the mirror. Yes, Frans was still Father, but the subconscious expectation that he would one day become her 'medical stallion' exerted its effects. She had to admit to herself that he was definitely not unattractive. Most of her friends thought he was thirty odd, so: much younger. A black voice whispered, "Why not, at first you didn't want Hans either and you fucked Jacob, though you didn't think much of him." A white voice whispered, "You can't do that, start an affair with her husband, your father, let alone fuck him." But the cry of distress from her second mouth, her vagina, sounded loudest, insistent and threatened to drown everything.

Frans too, sprayed himself with a scent - Armani - and was in doubt what to wear; a polo shirt, a black shirt, jeans ... Very different than before. He wanted to please, she wanted to please, subtle signs of a radical change in the father-daughter relationship.

One other evening than usual - a Tuesday - Frans rang at her door early in the evening. Ciska opened the front door in her Japanese kimono. Without make-up, without lipstick. She felt instantly ill at ease without any make-up.

Frans thought, as he kissed her on her proffered lips, "How young she looks without make-up, just like when she was fifteen. So young, so innocent, his little child." It gave him for an instant the weird titillation of abusing a child instead of flirting with his eighteen year old stepdaughter. And the conviction that her surrender was only a matter of time - days, weeks? - send tingles of anticipation through his flesh. There was no need to rush things. Ciska had to make up her mind. Her "itching" was his weapon.

They spoke little. They just enjoyed each other's company. As they were sitting on the sofa, Frans turned to her, kissed her and said softly, "I love you very much, you know. I think I'm falling in love with you." He blurted it out before he realized it. He was pleasantly surprised that she didn't blow the whistle on him by answering in a quasi-stern tone, "Don't be daft, your own daughter."

While Ciska was his aphrodisiac, or rather, his picture of her as his future lover, so the hormone androstenedione that raged through her body was Ciska's aphrodisiac. Like a randy cunt cries out to be satisfied, so her sexually plagued organ cried out for relief from the "sexual itch". At that moment she was like an eczema patient, crazy from the itching, who longs for the injection needle to be relieved from the suffering. Daddy's needle, as long as it works! Then the miracle happened before Frans' delighted gaze. With a tug she took off her kimono and lay stark naked on the Moroccan carpet. In less than no time Frans had taken off his clothes. The look of his Lolita, no older than fifteen, so childlike and yet so titillating, so sensual, was so overwhelming that associations from her childhood flashed back in his mind. Associations of Bashful and the night-kiss, the unfinished promise ten years ago.

Kneeling down near her face with his half-swollen penis near her mouth, Frans said hoarsely, "Cis, would you give Bashful a little kiss? You still love him, don't you, darling?" As he spoke Frans pressed his exposed glans against her lips. She started to suck at his member like on a lollipop, at first a bit insecure, but quickly greedily, while Frans prick, caressed by her tongue, grew bigger and harder triggered by the most delicious sensations., until he felt the soft pressure of her teeth rubbing his flesh as he started to fuck her orally: deep throat.

"Easy, Cis, he's very sensitive, "Frans whispered breathlessly, stopping his fucking movements, while Ciska, who had never performed fellatio before, started to suck even more eagerly. Sensing he was close to coming he withdrew his member with a jerk. Rearing like a stallion his enormous member bounced against his belly in front of his daughter's hazy gaze. "Don't come, daddy," Cis cried out in panic when she saw him struggling desperately to stop the ejaculation. He managed just in time.

"A cup of tea, Cis, to cool off a bit ?"As they were sitting naked on the couch with a hot mug of Rooibos tea, Cis on his lap, they watched a porno video Hans had bought in Zürich together with the high-tech vibrator. (At the time animal porno was not illegal) A woman with a Labrador . While Ciska watched, flushed, shocked but excited, as Frans was licking her brown erect nipple, he asked," Would you like to do it, Cis, fucking a dog?" [**Oh, the fantasy of men!**]

"It seems so scary, having sex with a dog." But his seismograph registered sweet tremors. Frans was so hot that he told her that Carrie, one of his many girlfriends over the years, whom Ciska knew, had fucked Daniel, their Danish dog on several occasions and had always found it terribly exciting. At his urgings she had even performed fellatio. He registered that the sight of the pale-red mucosa-covered penis, especially the close-up, excited her. "Would you try, Cis, just one time? Would be wonderful to see how Daniel fucks you. Perhaps you wouldn't be needing me anymore."

"Dad," she protested hotly, "all those awful diseases you can catch!"

"That's just the beauty of it, Cis. You can't get Aids and any other venereal infections from a dog because they don't take in humans. Moreover - even if you didn't wear a IUD - you could never get pregnant from a dog."

Oh, what kind of conversation between father and daughter, but at that moment Cis was his lover - that was the way it felt - who happened to be his daughter.

"I wouldn't dare, dad. Just imagine mom would find out!" she cried out in a flurry of guilt. "Do you know, your mother - I seduced her - had done it with Daniel for months till he jumped on her in company with a hard-on." Instantly he felt regret. He could have bitten off his tongue. Always loose-lipped when he was randy, a loose cannon. She jumped with a start, looking at him, "Dad, now you're talking bullshit." But from his expression, his body language, she could see he was speaking the truth. "Another rose balloon punctured," she sighed, feeling his peter, "Oh, he's getting hard again. Shall we?" It struck Frans that she referred to his organ as 'he' instead of it. He liked that.

"Gently, Cis, otherwise he'll come too soon." Cis dropped to her knees between daddy's thighs and, unasked, started to blow him again. Frans, half-randy, joked, "Looks like you're gnawing on a corncob, darling." She completed the analogy by pressing her teeth gently into his flesh. She looked up at him impishly. He had to laugh. Oh, they had such fun together ...

Unbelievable, Frans thought, yesterday unapproachable as a proper daughter, now his latest girlfriend. Frans was doubly excited by the sense that it was abnormal, perverse, taboo, just as he was twice as randy with Hans as with a woman by the fact that it was abnormal, perverse, making love to a boy, a man. At least that was his theory. Self-delusion?

Ciska was surprised that she was unashamedly sucking her father's cock, that she had almost fallen in love with it, while she had never wanted to perform fellatio on any of the other men - perhaps some forty - even with a condom. Unashamed, brazen, how could that be: father and lover all in one. He was her father, but sometimes more like her playmate, her closest friend. She realized clearly that she was crazy about him. He could be twenty-eight the way he looked undressed. She had fucked with guys as old as forty odd.

The next moment they both lay on the soft, white carpet, his head between her thighs, his delighted gaze close to his daughter's cunt, half-open, with her shapely lovely rose labia like petals of an opening rose covered with the dew of love. Oh, yesterday the picture, today the reality. The sight, the smell, the touch of his lips against her vaginal lips, all that was the sweetest experience of his life. Tenderness, romantic love, sexual desire, perhaps even parental love, all mixed in an intoxicating bliss that defied all description. But like the unseen Higgs field gives mass to all things - an ironic analogy - so the unseen GSA field gives love to the heart: sexual attraction. In an indirect manner Frans was influenced by the GSA field. Wasn't Ciska the product and the spitting image of Iris and Hans? Here, too, math is applicable: If A=B and B=C, then A=C. Translated, in words:

Frans felt attracted to Iris (F=I). Iris and Ciska were lookalike's (I=C), so Frans (though the father) was attracted to Ciska (F=C). True, but unthinkable, inconceivable.

Until this magical moment, born from the cauldron of Ciska's sexual despair. No wonder this was the loveliest moment in his memory.

Ciska was off the ground, she floated. The ceiling lamp transformed into the moon, the carpet into a flying carpet. And - miracle - the itching had gone; dancing butterflies in her stomach instead of burrowing moles down below. When the flying horse - her stallion - wanted to descend upon her, she whispered to his surprise, "No, Frans, don't, don't." This was the first time she called him by his name. "Why not, how about the itch?"

"The itch is gone. If you come in me I'm going to miss you too much."

He translated the message: "Then I'll love you too much."

Full of tenderness he lay down beside her. Kissing, entwined, they were lying on the flying carpet that carried them ever higher, ever further, to paradise ...

GSA Iris-Hans

28

Despite her anger, jealousy and humiliation on that dramatic night that Frans and Hans were '*glansing*' in her vagina (homo-activity) and Hans caught her fucking a dog, Iris stayed madly in love with Hans, comparable to Frans' passion for Hans.

More than once she'd told Frans, "Don't ask me to stop it, I can't." Frans understood: he couldn't stop with Hans either.

But while Frans as the 'leader' in the relationship with Hans was completely unhindered by inhibiting factors like shame, guilt, moral sense, etc. Iris was troubled by the admonishing voice of her conscience. Iris was the 'leader', since Hans was psychologically 'afraid' and 'submissive' (except in bed) with regard to his older sister and always assumed an expectant attitude towards Iris.

Periods of being madly in love with Hans and intense happiness alternated with long periods of self-disgust, depression, minor nervous breakdowns, as blue sky and heavy weather in the late summer. This and perhaps other factors in her character resulted over the years in a Iris-Hans affair that Frans metaphorically referred to as the oasis-desert relationship. Brief periods of completely being open to Hans' sexual desires alternating with long 'dry' desert periods, in which Iris closed up like a clam.

Was it self-protection, fear of addiction, fits of delusions, like the notion that her dead mother could see everything from the beyond? Neither Frans nor Hans could fathom it. In this regard she was totally unpredictable. Once Frans had made this ironic remark to Hans: "Iris and you both suffer from wind. While you let nature do its thing, Iris only occasionally passes a wind if she can't hold it up any longer. That's the difference between you and Iris."

The first three months after the 'dog-incident' were intense, divine. Oasis, in short. Iris wrote almost daily in her diary. Here is a passage.

We're in Holiday Inn in Leyden. The maid has hardly closed the door behind her or Hans and I taste each other's flesh. We both fall in our violent erotic world. I bite his neck. Hans let me lie down with legs spread wide and bores into me. That my brother fucks me excites me madly. Our appetites are boundless I love him to distraction. "Oh, Iris, did Frans taught you that? But you can fuck, you can fuck, I'm crazy about you. I'm yours, now and forever."

"I'm crazy about you, too." And then I say something that surprises me. "It is not only the fucking is it? You do love me, don't you, darling?" The doubt, the need for his love, the romantic love of my own brother, my own blood. Incest! Oh, what a shame! But what a gorgeous experience to be madly in love with your favourite brother, the forbidden fruit. Only odd that it makes no difference to him, with his sister. "You're simply a beautiful woman. The woman of my wet dreams." Does Hans really love me or is it just all about sex. I'm head over heels in love with him. Oh, if it ever gets out ...

Except the 'desert-oasis' situation originating from Iris brain, there was something else. She was often morbidly jealous with regard to Hans. Especially when she found out they - Frans and Hans - had sex in her absence, like when they had switched their underpants by mistake, or, when Iris caught them once in *flagrante delicto* in their summer house. Hysterically she had chased the frightened lovers naked out of the cottage, a bit like Jesus in the Temple. Totally unlike her normal self. Furious she had thrown their clothes after them. Crying and choking with jealousy she had driven home and hadn't spoken to Frans for a week. Before her affair with her brother she had also been very angry and emotional when she had surprised them on one or two occasions. But this reaction was a hundred times worse: really morbid compared to her 'normal' outburst of anger.

But Iris couldn't help it. This is a familiar symptom of the GSA condition (genetic sexual attraction): violent jealousy.

An interview in the Guardian (May 17, 2003) with a GSA 'victim' about his affair with his adopted sister (whom he'd never known as a child) mentions: *he became intensely jealous, an emotion, he stresses, that had been alien to him.*

Even during his sex fantasies in bed, often based on real erotic experiences, Iris got annoyed when he told her about things that happened between him and Hans only weeks ago. Stories that happened months ago were OK: that was history and aroused no undue jealousy.

Unrelated to her affair with her brother Iris had another peculiar weakness: **amnesia with regard to her own extra-marital affairs.**

As mentioned earlier Iris and Hans had opted, a few years after their wedding, for an "open marriage". A boyfriend (girlfriend) was OK, within limits, of course. Iris didn't act jealous about Frans' affairs as long as she was in love, had a boyfriend.

But, oh, when that was not the case. Then Frans was a 'bastard', fooling around with other women and she would spend nights venting her spleen on Frans and that 'bitch' to Edith, a friend.

Frans didn't have these negative feelings, whether or not he had a girlfriend when Iris was having an affair. Yes, Iris, when she was 'single' and he was having an affair would hurl the most awful reproaches at him and choked with jealousy. But Iris wasn't a saint either, as these two examples illustrate.

Iris had fallen seriously in love with Alex, a cheeky, cheerful, trendy lad who was busy building up his electronics emporium at 33, a swinger she'd met in the VOOM-VOOM, a trendy disco on one of the canals in Amsterdam.

One day Frans had to give a lecture in Nijmegen, a town some 60 miles away and would be home at around one a.m.

He knew that Alex would be fucking Iris in their nuptial bed. No problem! But Alex must leave before one o'clock for he would be dead tired and wanted to go to bed immediately. Iris promised. To his great annoyance he had to spend an hour waiting in his study below the bedroom listening to their banter, moans and other noises.

Since Frans hated confrontations he had not stormed into the bedroom like in a Hollywood scene. Iris was having sex in their nuptial bed while he was at home. That he would never have dreamt of doing when Iris was at home or close.

Another example. Our Alex, by now owner of a chain of electronic stores and top distributor of Philips articles, received, like the twenty other top sellers, an invitation from Philips for a *deluxe* boat trip on the Rhine with his wife. Iris came along under the guise of being his wife. Frans had no problems with it. Very adventurous and a bit extreme, even for a free marriage.

But when Frans 'had done something' it never occurred to Iris to think, 'I haven't been such an angel either'. She always acted the injured innocent, he was the adulterer.

Also, during the "desert-periods" Iris was completely inaccessible to Hans' timid advances, despite Frans' encouragements and bed fantasies. In that respect she seemed a bit 'schizoid': light on or off, nothing in-between.

Had the GSA been turned off in the desert-periods? Even the psychiatrist was unable to answer this question when she was in therapy years later. Maybe the self-control of her higher 'ego' was so strong that she had her windiness well under control. One thing was certain. Hans suffered terribly in silence during these unpredictable periods in the desert. The dream to fuck his sister, to kiss her 'divine' cunt had been realized and had raised his sexual desire to fever pitch. Oh, the frustration and pangs of love when she was again suddenly inaccessible, a marble statue of Venus.

To illustrate the nature of the Iris-Hans on-and-off relationship over the years the chronicler presents three events that offer an impression of the unnatural relationship between brother and sister.

Caught 1

It had been desert time for over a year. Frans and Hans had thought up a plan to fan the fire of her smouldering passion. Frans would go with Iris to a wellness centre where Hans happened to be present. Seeing her brother naked may have exerted a positive influence on her latent, suppressed feelings for her brother, as the following incident leads one to suspect. A few weeks after the sauna encounter Frans and Hans were having sex in the summer house, convinced that the coast was clear. They were both terrified of Iris since her latest outburst.

When Hans and Frans were lying on the couch half-undressed, Hans with his head resting on the arm rest, Frans with his head between Hans' thighs they suddenly heard the front door being opened. They were petrified and Frans thought it was the cleaning woman. Frans called out in panic, "Don't come in, don't come in."

The door opened and Iris stood in the doorway. Bewildered the two sinners looked up from their lowly position and expected a repeat of the Temple scene. To their relief and surprise she remained silent and sat on the plastic 'pilot-chair' near the door behind Hans' head resting on the armrest. She watched with a Mona Lisa smile on her lips. They realized they had nothing to fear and Frans started blowing Hans again while Iris was watching. She threw up her skirt, pulled her briefs down and began to masturbate. Hans, his head in his neck looked avidly at the wonderful scene: his sister watching them while she was fingering. Her pubic hair was visible, that was all.

Frans felt Hans' penis 'rearing' in his mouth. Ultimate excitement. Frans pulled his mouth back and said, "Iris don't you think he's gorgeous. Will you kiss your brother's lovely dick?"

But she made no movement and lisped, fingering even faster, "No, you just carry on." Iris did not participate in any way, except baring her pussy to Hans' delighted gaze.

Iris saw Hans coming in Frans' mouth and very deliberately Frans repeatedly withdrew his mouth to show Iris the semen eruptions. While Hans, moaning with 'double' pleasure was coming Iris had a spasmodic orgasm as she fingered with the amazing pace of a sowing machine, her briefs on the floor, her super-randy swollen labia exposed to her brother's lewd gaze. In his excitement Frans kissed Hans on his mouth, his mouth full of Hans' sperm. Iris left shortly after. At the front door Hans was allowed to give her a parting kiss.

That night in bed Iris asked Frans, "Did Hans bring you off while I was in the toilet?"

"No, why?"

"I tasted seed as he gave me a kiss."

"That was Hans' semen. He came in my mouth and then I kissed him. You tasted your brother's semen, darling, isn't it exciting?"

It was: the start of a new oasis period. Alas, too brief...

Caught 2

Some years later the following incident occurred which throws some light on Frans latent jealousy with regard to the Hans-Iris relationship.

It was a fine summer evening. Frans and Iris were visiting Hans and Sacha, his wife. The ladies were drinking wine, Hans whiskey, Frans a cognac. Iris got a bit merry and a bit naughty. The way she flirted with her eyes with Hans ever so often when Sacha wasn't looking. It was not the oasis period, but the lush desert grass, the lone palm tree and the succulent cactuses proclaimed the presence of the oasis at the horizon. At one point the conversation was about bio-resonance therapy. Iris said it had done her a lot of good: more energy, better sleep and no more headaches. Sacha was keenly interested as she had been feeling rather tired and droopy lately. Frans who, besides his aeronautical work for Airbus and other companies, ran - like quite a few hard scientists - a small alternative practice, as earlier, suggested to drive to his office in Woerden, some 20 miles away, for a bio-resonance treatment. He had an ulterior motive. It would be a good opportunity to screw Sacha, he fancied that. They had had sex a few times and though Sacha was no beauty she was very nice and - for Frans - definitely not sexually unattractive. Hans had been left in the dark, since as a 'white Arab' (Dubai), "he could do anything, she was allowed nothing", not even going to the bar of the Amsterdam-Hilton with her girlfriend when he was in the Middle-East for months.

When Sacha hesitated, Iris said, "Yes, Sacha, why don't you, It will make you feel so much better."

Iris wanted to be alone with Hans, the wine had stirred her latent erotic desires. For Frans it was as plain as a pikestaff.

Frans and Sacha were on the motorway when she said, "Turn back. I forgot my lipstick. Otherwise Hans will notice it." Frans got a fright for he knew or suspected that Hans and Iris, feeling secure, would be having at least a nice cuddle by now. He had felt it from the atmosphere. Frans wanted to continue driving but Sacha was in a state. She wanted nothing better than go to bed with Frans, but … "Then I can't go to bed with you, for if Hans sees me without lipstick …" So Frans had little choice but turn round. But he would have done better to think, "Well better no sex than Sacha catching them in the act." Was it the little demon of jealousy in the dark regions of his sub-consciousness, a certain sadistic vindictiveness, masochism, thirst for sensation, that drove him?

"Stop here," Sacha said. It was near the gate of the large garden bordering the street. Sacha walked along the swimming pool to the house where Hans and Iris were sitting on the terrace. On a wide couch, each in a corner, Iris, apparently a bit under the influence, had kicked off her shoes and was sitting, her back against the armrest, with one folded leg on the couch, her bare toe provocatively near his fly. She laughed defiantly, a bit randy.

Sacha, afraid to be seen, ran back to the car. She was completely shaken. "I'm sure those two are having an affair," she stammered between tears. She wanted to get out of the car, have another look, but Frans started the engine and drove off at high speed. Better a suspicion than certitude, he thought magnanimously. But the damage had already been done. Sacha was sitting with a contorted face and posture, eyes closed, deep in thought. Now she understood why Hans was so often not in the mood for sex. *He's having an affair with his sister.* When she told Frans about it he felt a bit relieved. Hans and he had sex almost every week and Hans and

Iris only occasionally in their on-off relationship. He was the cause of Hans 'impotence' towards Sacha, not Iris. But he was off the hook for now, a liberating thought.

If Frans had not driven away, Sacha would have seen how Iris with her green polished big toe had playfully approached his crotch till Hans opened his fly. How her toe caressed his glans, how she got up to take off her briefs to show her rose swollen labia to her brother's delighted gaze. Then the curtain would fall as they left the stage - the terrace - to proceed to the order of the night.

The parting

Hans had to go to Finland for a few days for his work. Iris and Frans had a meal with him in Hoofddorp near Schiphol on the night of his departure. It was the early start of a new oasis period. Iris had glammed herself up. She was wearing Hans' favourite dress, short, fiery red, with puff sleeves and a plunging neckline. And the expensive pearl necklace Hans had bought her in Dubai. Once again Iris was head over heels in love with Hans. Frans thought it was great, despite a pang of jealousy. After the meal during which the love birds were sitting next to each other and Iris felt his fly occasionally, they walked to the deserted parking place packed with cars. Hans would drive to Schiphol in his own car. They bid Hans farewell at Frans' Jaguar. Iris was leaning against the door. Hans kissed his sister. He was allowed to fondle her breasts and in the pale artificial lighting Frans saw Hans pulling down her dress shoulder, greedily kissing her nipple while she, blissfully happy, eyes closed, allowed him to carry on. Frans, kneeling, giving Hans a blow job, had a great time. As Hans got into his car he cried out with a hot face, "Iris, I want to screw you."

"If it's all right with Frans," she shouted back. The hypocrite.

Three weeks later Hans had again to go to Dubai for an extended period: three months. Sacha took him to Schiphol. They bid each other farewell at the revolving door of the departure hall.

A bit later Iris and Hans met in the lounge of the Schiphol-Hilton where she had booked a room. While Sacha 'knew' Hans was sleeping on the plane, he was sleeping with his sister in the bridal suite of Schiphol-Hilton.

The good example

30

It looked like she was very much in love. With her own father. But in her perception Frans felt less and less like 'daddy' and more and more as her new boyfriend. Although she tried to suppress it Cis did have a guilty conscience. *You can't do that, having a secret affair with your father, your mother's husband.*

But the erotic attraction - in her case also a kind of shadow-GSA-effect - was too strong. Two things had struck Frans. Very soon she no longer called him 'daddy' or 'Aapje' (little monkey), but 'Frans'. It seemed to come naturally. The second thing was her pubic hair, till now characterized by the juvenile shape of a flattened ellipse, that had within three months reached the adult form: the inverse triangle. Biologically almost impossible that fast. Because of her crush the hormones raged through her body and had quickly made up arrears.

Three months later she was no longer daddy's little girl but a (very) young grown-up woman, thanks to the 'romance' and her hormones.

Frans, the only person who knew that she was not his biological daughter, had - maybe in order to assuage his bad conscience - hazy fantasies about the Woody Allen-Soon-Yi affair [Soon-Yi, his step daughter from his marriage with Mia Farrow, whom he later married]. There was in fact nothing illegal about their affair: Ciska was in fact his step daughter (DNA was the proof), not a next of kin but related by marriage. According to the law he could even marry her. *Woody Allen!*

He regretted he was unable to share this secret with Ciska, but that was of course out of the question. As Frans and Ciska had agreed, they never touched one another in public; not the slightest suggestion of eroticism. *One never knows.*

Ciska had told her mother that she would draw the curtains from now on because of a peeping Tom, and that she had a new boyfriend, Fons Kraan, a journalist, married. She knew Iris didn't think much of him. So, that would keep Iris at a safe distance in the evenings! Frans came twice a week or they had sex in a motel. Ciska was no longer interested in boys and her itching was now a thing of the past. To his own surprise Frans neglected his two current girlfriends, Eva and Inge. Only with Yvonne he had sex on a regular basis and this was the reason of the ultimate orgy in which Ciska was closely involved, shortly before their fatal trip to the Far East.

As the sex-orientation test in the hospital (AMC) had shown Frans was exclusively hetero, with homo-interest only for improbably beautiful boys - 'feminine' but not 'effeminate' - seventeen and older, the kind of person you never meet in real life. But this 'medical prediction' would soon pass the test of reality with flying colours.

Yvonne

Years earlier Frans had met Yvonne at a party in Bloemendaal (near Haarlem). They hit it off immediately and during their first meal Frans told her, "If I hadn't been married, I would have liked to marry you. I say this just as an expression of my feelings for you." At the time Yvonne was thirty-two - she married early but was divorced - and had two children, a daughter of twelve and a son of ten. She was very pretty, very sexy and had been an actress since leaving high school at sixteen until she joined KLM at twenty-eight. Cheeky, brazen and yet a bit childlike, she exuded sex-appeal, a bit like Marilyn Monroe, her idol. Wearing her auburn hair in a bob gracing her naughty angelic features, Yvonne was for Frans, with her slender figure and small, firm breasts perhaps the most alluring of his numerous girlfriends over the years. Anyway he was smitten.

Although she'd loved her husband to distraction she had left him because of his alcoholism and perhaps the emotional emptiness since her divorce was the cause of her sexual depravity. Frans and Yvonne were lovers and had no (sexual) secrets for each other and because of his infatuation Yvonne was more than usual the target of Iris' jealousy and anger.

Yvonne had told Frans that she had blowed Frits, the seven year old child of her best friend, a KLM stewardess like her. The boy had cried out, "Auntie Yvonne, how dirty you're." It had become a kind of addiction, that Frits seemed to enjoy. In those days - the eighties - paedophilia wasn't yet on the political agenda in the Netherlands, so she could 'permit herself' to have sex even with her own kids (boy and girl), like fellatio with her son, but always through 'seduction', never under pressure. In short, a perfect shambles.

Because the testicles of her son had not descended yet into the scrotum and Yvonne, rightly, was seriously worried (risk: sterility because of the high body temperature) Frans had treated Wim with LH-injections, the pituitary hormone that promotes the descent of the testicles into the scrotum. This, his friend Roel, the gynaecologist, had strongly advised. By giving the extra high dose (5000 IU pregnyl, instead of the standard dose of 3000 IU, three times a week) not only the testicles had quickly descended, but the at that age very 'hormone-sensitive' peter had expanded to a size greater than 30% of normal in the drooping state.

A few years later when Wim was seventeen his penis was over eighteen cm during erection, considerably longer than the average length of fourteen and a half cm to which Frans penis conformed. Just like a small penis repels, an oversized penis arouses sexual desire in women. Here our story begins and we're back in the here and now.

When one day (night) Frans and Yvonne were making love in the summer house she told him the following story. She was at the time living in a small house with her two children, Wim, seventeen and her daughter, nineteen.

It was heavy weather; thunder and lightning all during the night. At times the whole room was illuminated by lightning. Yvonne was really terrified, perhaps also because she'd seen their home burnt to the ground as a child. Without any ulterior motive, she awoke her son to ask him to join her in her bed. In the early morning (he wore only a T-shirt, she told Frans) she awoke and saw his morning erection.

She got so excited by the look of his 'oversized' member that she felt a strong urge to squat on top of him and fuck him, she confided. The next night, too, she wanted him to stay with her, despite the presence of her daughter, who, for that matter, gave little comment.

She knew Yvonne who was a little bit crazy anyway. In her excitement Yvonne tried to seduce him to perform 'the act'. Just when she thought she'd got him to fuck her he'd protested, despite his swishing peter, "Oh, no, that's impossible! With your mother."

Yes, mother was still young and attractive, but however much she tried - she had even masturbated him to near orgasm - all to no avail. He did kiss her nipple, but fucking ... No, that was impossible. Taboo. When Frans asked her: "Did you perform fellatio?", she said, "No, I didn't dare." Fellatio with her son - now since he was almost a grown-up - Yvonne was more ashamed of than fucking.

Frans, who was looking for sensation thought it was a wonderful story and when she saw he was interested she asked him if he would perhaps have a chat with Wim to convince him with proper arguments that sometimes sex between mother and son was OK (mother divorced, no risk of pregnancy, etc.). Frans had told Yvonne about a book published by the French Society for Sexual Reform which contained a great number of positive personal experiences told either by the mother or the son about mother-son sex. "Would you translate some of it and read it to Wim?" Yvonne had asked.

Frans was quite willing to mediate but first he wanted to see a picture of Wim. It was too long ago. At their next meeting Yvonne showed some pictures. Frans was amazed. What a looker: ugly duckling transformed into a swan! Wim wore long hair with a pony from the seventies which gave him the look of a good-looking athletic young female.

"Yes, that's right," Yvonne affirmed, "the doctors in AMC [Amsterdam Medical Centre] have found that he is in fact intersexual."

"What? A hermaphrodite?"

"No, you can't use that term anymore. He is a man, but they have found ovaries and he has some breast development like a thirteen year old girl."

Frans continued to gaze in fascination at the picture, also the one on the beach. '*A hermaphrodite with a supersized penis,*' he concluded as he studied the picture on the beach. Intersexual: that explained the curious attraction these pictures exerted on him.

Wim was a good draughtsman, but was mentally a bit below average, not at all retarded but a bit of a Simple Simon. According to tests he was best suited for artist or technical draughtsman. He was very shy with girls and never had a girlfriend.

As an unnatural father but a natural lover it seemed to Frans a good idea that Ciska should be present at his attempt to convince Wim that it was sometimes OK to have sex with your parent of the opposite sex. Ciska would serve as the living example. Fortunately Ciska was not jealous of his girlfriends and she had met Yvonne before. She thought she was very nice. It took Frans little effort to persuade Ciska to go along with him. "Oh, how exciting! I do hope you'll bring it off. Then I know in any case I'm not the only one," she gushed.

Wim was home alone. His sister was on vacation in the Ardennes with her boyfriend. The first thing Wim said as he opened the front door was, "Hey, you haven't changed one bit, uncle Frans!"

"You have, Wim. I really wouldn't have recognized you. Good heavens, how you have changed!"

Frans was amazed. Wim looked even more handsome (the term 'beautiful' applies) than in the pictures.

And - this struck him as odd - he was not male but not female either. Something in-between? No, neither. More something very different, undefinable. As a mathematician Frans immediately conjured up a triangle with male in the left corner, female in the right and Wim at the top. So, elsewhere. Later the medical report at AMC showed that Wim was not XY, but XX, so biologically a woman. But how can a female have a peter and many other characteristics of a male? The interested reader will find the complex answer in the frame below.

> As everyone knows the male is XY (the cells contain both the male chromosome Y and the female chromosome X). The Y chromosome contains (don't be alarmed) the SRY gene. This gene determines that the foetus will become a boy. It acts as a trigger that opens up hundreds of genes (on DNA) to form a penis, etc. But in rare cases (1 in 20,000) the SRY gene is by 'translocation' located on a X chromosome, by which the XX individual is not a female but a male. This is known as 'de La Chapelle syndrome', after the doctor who discovered it.
>
> This was the case with Wim, but a further complication was that besides testicles in the scrotum (after proper descent) doctors had discovered ovarian tissue in the abdomen. Wim was a hermaphrodite, a term referring to Greek mythology where the God Hermaphroditus was both male and female by 'merging' with a nymph. Wim was medically such a unique case that he was often presented at medical meetings, even abroad. What surprised the specialists most was how this XX-SRY positive individual could have such a large penis and healthy fertile sperm. The XX-males are sterile and have a small penis. *The result of pregnyl injections,* but that was a family secret. Only in 2013 in Germany intersexuality was officially recognized as a separate category, like 'male' and 'female'.

Both Frans and Ciska were very surprised about Wim's 'exotic' beauty and aura. Ciska later said, "He looks almost like an angel." Hermaphroditus was (in Greek mythology) a God and the Greek historian Diodorus Siculus (first century B.C.) wrote:

Some say that this Hermaphroditus was a God and at certain times appeared among humans and that he's born with a physical body that is a combination of that of a man and of a woman, in the sense that he has a body that is beautiful and delicate like that of a woman, but possesses the masculine qualities, power and penis of a man.

With his 'angelic features', hair dress of the seventies, long dark eye lashes, flame-coloured lips and gentle, amiable disposition Wim exerted a mysterious erotic influence on Frans, an influence he had - except with Hans – never experienced before. And there was that faint recollection of that funny kid with whom he had flown kites in the dunes five years ago.

After some chit-chat and an explanation how Frans and Ciska had fallen in love as a result of her 'itching problem' (*all very hush-hush*) Frans, with Ciska at his side, came to the point. Apparently Wim didn't feel embarrassed by Ciska's presence.

Here are a few snippets of their conversation.

"Do you know Yvonne wants to go to bed with you?"

"Yes, I know, but with your mother, that's impossible, isn't it?"

"Just be honest, Wim, do you think Yvonne is beautiful?"

"I've always found my mother very attractive."

"Do you sometimes think of her when you frig off?"

He blushed, shot a glance at Ciska, but admitted he did.

"Remember, Wim, when you still lived in Zandvoort [Holland's famous bathing resort near Amsterdam] you sometimes had to sleep in Yvonne's bed under some pretext and that Yvonne would suck your peter?"

Wim remembered everything in full detail.

"One time Yvonne was sitting on top of me."

He nearly always called her Yvonne, rarely mom.

"With your prick in her cunt?"

"Yes."

"Was it nice. You remember?"

"It was a randy feeling, but at the same time I thought it odd what she did. Fucking your own child."

"Yes, Yvonne told that me she found it terribly exciting, your stiff little peter in her pussy. But now she longs even much more to feel your big hard-on in her cunt. The incest taboo only goes for a married couple because of the rivalry between son and father, and besides, Yvonne can no longer get pregnant. She has been sterilized, you know that, don't you? Yvonne is very impressed by your large peter. Women are crazy about that."

"Yes, I know, sometimes she stands behind me naked under the shower to soap me."

"Also your prick?"

"Yes, especially."

"And then what? Do you get a hard-on?"

"What do you think?" Frans saw he had a half-erection from the 'tent' at his fly.

Frans said Yvonne had told him she once had hidden the key of his room so she could surprise him when she knew he was jacking off.

"Yes, I was scared to death. I felt so embarrassed the first time. But she touched me and bared her nipple to make me even hotter."

As Frans had promised Yvonne he read a number of stories he had translated from the book of the French society for sexual reform. They were reports by members, anonymous, of course, about mother-son sex, some written by the mother, others by the son. All experiences were very positive, satisfying ...

Wim's problem was not that he didn't find Yvonne attractive (he often fantasied about her when he jerked himself off) but because he thought fucking your mother was simply wrong.

Wim and Ciska had been listening in rapt attention and Frans got the impression that the stories had given him a different look on things.

The curtains were drawn. Frans saw from Ciska's flushed cheeks and the brilliance in her shrouded eyes that she too felt the electricity.

"So you see, Wim, sex between mother and son happens often enough and is in fact very natural, only one doesn't talk about it, like you don't talk about frigging off, do you? By the way, have you ever fucked a girl?"

"No, never," Wim answered, blushing.

"Now then, you surely must do it with Yvonne at least once, even if it were only for the wonderful experience of coming gloriously in a randy cunt. You really have no idea what you're missing, Wim."

Frans felt he'd really talked him round, but only knew it for sure when Wim asked, "But if Nicole [his sister] finds out?" *Mission accomplished.*

The next theme . It seemed like Frans and Wim had been oblivious of Ciska' s presence, perhaps because she was such a self-effacing person, not somebody who is emphatically present like her mother, Iris.

"Remember, Wim, those injections I gave you to let you balls descent into your scrotum? Yvonne asked me to examine whether your balls have really fully descended, and whether your semen is OK. I have to send it to the lab for testing."

At the time Frans had been wearing a white coat (from his lab) to give the fearful little boy the impression that he was a doctor. Wim still thought he was.

Frans extracted a vial from his pocket and said, "Later you have to jerk yourself off in the toilet and collect your seed for the lab."

Again Frans told Wim that Yvonne lusted after his big peter. He told him that this was the result of the hormone injections, as he - to make sure - had given him more than the standard dose.

Frans and Wim were sitting on the couch, Ciska on the piano stool.

"I would like to see the result, Wim. It's purely medical and I have to measure the size of your balls and your peter, too," Frans said, playing doctor to perfection as he took out the tape and two medical instruments and placed them on the coffee table.

"Does it have to be now," he asked nervously, shooting a glance at Ciska." Yes, Wim purely medical."

"Cis, go and watch TV upstairs, darling." Obedient as a little girl Ciska left the room. "I'll call you when we're done," Frans called after her.

"Open your fly," the doctor ordered. Nervously, Wim pulled his zipper down.

"Show ..."

Frans didn't wait but pulled Wim's rod from his fly. For a long moment Frans stared in surprise. It was almost twice as big as Hans', or so it appeared. Frans felt a strong urge to touch, pull back his foreskin, kiss his glans, but he controlled himself. With professional *gravitas* he started to carry out the measurements after

Wim had dropped his pants and underpants at his request so as to expose his balls too.

"Sorry, Wim but I have to touch you a bit to measure your balls and your peter."

He underwent the examination passively. They didn't speak.

"Do you know your peter is almost twice as big as normal?" Frans said with some exaggeration. No, he didn't, for, except as a little kid, he had never seen another boy naked.

Frans pulled his own half-erect member out of his pants. "Look, this is the normal size. You see the difference? And besides, mine is half-hard and yours still limp. Now I understand why Yvonne is in love with your dick. Women love big peters, also in their cunts."

Suddenly Frans realized that this was the first male - boy - except Hans, who exerted an erotic influence on him.

His foreskin appeared a bit narrow. Frans, the 'doctor', looking professional, asked if it bothered him when he had a hard-on. He said it squeezed a bit.

"Can you pull it down completely past your glans when you're beating off?"

Frans grabbed his penis and pushed the foreskin gently backwards up and down, supposedly to check for *phimosis* (too narrow foreskin, like Hans before the operation). Wim allowed it and he seemed to like it. In fact Frans was masturbating him under the pretence of ... Frans still had his member in his trousers and Wim saw Frans was quickly getting an erection.

"Hey, are you getting randy, uncle Frans?" he asked cheekily.

"Just call me Frans," Frans said in a husky voice.
Frans stopped for a moment masturbating Wim.
"Why do you stop?" he breathed.

"You know what. I'll give your prick a lovely feeling, almost as nice as in a cunt." He bended over and started to kiss Wim's excitingly large penis. Wim was over the moon from the new sensation of fellatio. He kept moaning, "Oh, how lovely, this is much better than jerking off."

Frans said, "Be blown is nice, but fucking is even better." And for Yvonne's sake he explained, "A cunt is wonderful, tight and juicy and especially the cunt's muscles are fantastic. A cunt is like my tongue: all muscle.; it's as if a hundred tongues are licking your cock instead of one, like this one." And Frans' tongue began slurping, sucking, with doubled passion and enjoyment at his by now extremely sensitive glans, ready to explode at any moment.

"You really mean it, you really, mean it, uncle Frans?"

"Frans" he corrected. "Yes, really, makes sense, for your cock is made for a cunt, not for a hand or a mouth. A blow job is just a foretaste for the bliss of a cunt. You realize now what good luck you have that Yvonne wants to fuck you? Go for it. Leap at the chance!"

Wim, very shy with girls despite his beauty and sex-appeal, was now completely won over, hooked. He wanted nothing better than that experience, be it with his own mother.

Ciska had been so engrossed in an exciting soap that she'd lost all sense of time or space. The doorbell chimed four times. It was Yvonne, but Frans had not told Wim. He was scared stiff.

Frans said, "It is Yvonne, you really don't have to be ashamed for she knows we would have sex and besides she is sexually in love with you. Maybe you can fuck her now already, isn't that wonderful, Wim? But first I'm going to fuck your mother, here on the floor while you watch."

In his excitement Frans had forgotten all about Ciska. Frans walked to the front door. Yvonne saw his hard-on. With a conspiratorial look she stepped across the doorstep. "Feel like it, darling? Wim is all in the mood."

Wim was sitting on the couch and looked a bit anxiously and uncertainly at his mother. She sat beside him, kissed him hard on the mouth and felt his half-erect peter. In less than no time Yvonne was naked. Frans and Yvonne were lying on the carpet as Frans started kissing her pussy while Wim was watching. He jerked her belly towards the couch so that Wim could see her moist rose cunt.

"Look, Wim, your mother's cunt; that's where you came from, that's where you enter." While Wim watched breathlessly as Frans and Yvonne were making love Yvonne looked, her head turned sideways, at Wim's enormous peter beating against his pubic hair, while her belly was shaking wildly under Frans deep thrusts.

"Look Wim, that's the way you should fuck your mother. Your mother lusts for your divine cock, don't you, Yvonne?"

Frans stopped abruptly and said, "Wim, fuck your mother."

Naked, Wim jumped his mother almost like a rapist, with the instinctive lewdness of a he-dog jumping a bitch in heat. While mother and son, moaning, kissing, wildly shaking, were making love, Frans, masturbating, watched Yvonne's buttocks rise into the air as her son bore deep into her flesh and they fused in consanguine love. "Wim, "she cried out in ecstasy, "I want your seed, I want your seed in my cunt. I want your wonderful seed, the seed of my own son, my boy." She just kept jabbering away in her state of divine oblivion.

At that moment the door opened and Ciska stood in the doorway. They came at the same time. Yvonne at the moment that she knew Wim was coming. An explosion of lewdness, emotion, bliss, love and pleasure. Frans tore the clothes from his daughter, threw her on the couch and fucked his daughter, while mother and son, heavy but intensely happy, watched entwined the father fucking his own daughter.

Later Wim told Yvonne, "I was so glad to see Frans fucking his daughter. That's much better than all those French stories. At least now I know I'm not the only one."

Wim's words were echoed by Ciska's remark to her daddy:

"Dad, I'm so glad I was present when Wim was fucking his mother. At least now I know I'm not the only one. You know, this means much more to me than all those stories about Woody Allen."

Frans had to laugh inwardly. *Do as you would be done by.* He arranged it for Yvonne and now Ciska has been cured of her (taboo) 'complex'. Except for those feelings of guilt towards her mother. But after all: what the eye doesn't see the heart doesn't grieve over. Like his affair with Hans he's been able to hide from Iris for years.

Far East

31

In order not to raise suspicion Ciska went (supposedly) with a friend (girl) to Nepal ten days earlier. But in fact she was staying with her friend in Groningen, some 100 miles north of Amsterdam. Frans would go on his own - so, without a girlfriend - to the Far East: Thailand, Singapore, Bali, Hong Kong, as he had done before. He knew Iris wouldn't offer to accompany him, as she abhorred 'all that poverty'. Frans and Ciska travelled by Singapore Airlines.

In her high spirits Ciska occasionally displayed traits of an adolescent, the way she squatted on the trolley Frans was laboriously pushing at Schiphol, and the way Ciska responded when the stewardess tucked her in for the night. But when the lights dimmed the mature woman awakened: she blew Frans and allowed him to finger her and kiss her nipple. They were besotted and simply couldn't leave each other alone.

The vacation passed in love and harmony, except for that evening in Manila when Frans wanted to call Iris at her insistence as he'd promised. Ciska's reaction surprised him. She tore the receiver from his hand and ranted and raved hysterically. "I'm calling your mother, not a girlfriend," he said, baffled.

"We're on vacation together!" she cried overwrought," I don't want to share you with anyone!" He just went ahead and that evening and the next day they hardly spoke to each other. Frans consoled himself with the thought, *'She must be crazy about me.'* She was his Soon-Yi, only she didn't know she was his step-daughter. But even if she did, did they have a future?

Like postcards and tweets offer a glimpse of a nice vacation, the following snippets present the same function.

- In the blue waters of Phuket they made love surrounded by a sea of jellyfish.

- In a sex-tent in Bangkok they watched a woman under loud cheering shoot a Cola bottle from her athletic vagina into the admiring crowd.

- Ciska, three days very ill with diarrhoea from an infection, was too weak to stand or walk. In the beach bungalow they slept in separate beds. When she'd to pee during the night she would throw a pillow to Frans, who would carry her as a little child to the toilet. Thanks to antibiotics she was completely recovered on day four.

- On the beach in Bali, on a pitch-dark night, Ciska pointed at the sky and said "Look." For 20 minutes they watched in amazement three lights cutting the most impossible capers. Frans, the scientist, who had never believed in UFO's, was converted.

- They were trapped for hours at the top of a Ferris wheel in Shenzhen, Communist China (it was the early eighties) because of a power failure.

- Just as that night with Hans, Frans had come six times. The next day he walked with a limp and shooting aches in his groin as Holland's greatest sexologist Dr. van der Velde had 'predicted' nearly a hundred years ago.

- In Bali when they walked back to the beach hotel after a delicious Indonesian meal Ciska cried in panic, "A snake!" Instead of protecting Ciska, take her in his arms, Frans dashed away the moment he saw the python slither in front of his feet.

- In the disco of the Manila Hyatt Hotel they received the *Saturday Night Fever Award* on the dance floor as they collapsed in each other's arms.

- It had struck Ciska that no one - not even taxi drivers - saw them as father and daughter, but as a couple. It meant a lot to her.

*

It was their last evening. They were sitting in the French restaurant *Lalique* of the 5-star hotel *Shangri-La* that had recently opened its doors.

Ciska felt like Cinderella in these exotic surroundings with the love of her life at her side. She was sitting in silent enjoyment and took in the scene with a sense of well-being: the polished black panelling, interrupted by alcoves ablaze with light, full of multi-coloured *Lalique* glass-and crystal ware, the club chairs, some in green damask, others in black leather, the floral-patterned Bordeaux-red Chinese carpet, the immense windows providing a view of Hong Kong Harbour and its thousands of lights from junks to enormous cruise ships.

The whole, the dimmed lighting, the buzz of well-bred voices in all tongues was perfect for their last meal before they would leave for Schiphol the next day.

Ciska's heart was filled with a mixture of bliss and vague *tristesse*.

Bliss in the PRESENT, sadness at the thought of TOMORROW. Almost three weeks they had been together day and night, free, without fear of prying eyes.

Ciska had never felt so happy and safe, in the arms of his love and their intimate togetherness. TOMORROW everything would be different again: twice a week a few snatched hours together. The mere thought was unbearable and brought her to the verge of despair. More than ever she knew on this final day that she wanted nothing better than to be always together. In her daydreams she even fantasized that she fled with Frans to Tahiti or some other exotic island; to paradise: together forever.

Her infatuation was the result of a curious interplay of three factors: the indirect influence of GSA, shadow-GSA: her genes were virtually identical to those of Iris. No wonder she could potentially fall in love with the same man as Iris.

The erotic sexual-tinted experience with Bashful had deeply affected her love life and its orientation. And last but not least the 'sexual itching', the factor that transformed everything that was latently present into reality.

To what extent the fact that Frans was not her biological father also played a role is a question even the Gods couldn't answer.

Frans too was sad at the thought that this was their final day. He was so crazy about this enchanting 'new girlfriend', who happened to be his daughter, that he wanted nothing better than being inseparably together forever. His shining example was Woody Allen, his hero.

"Can't we just stay here, in Bali, Tahiti? I always want to be with you, darling," Ciska imagined, holding his hand. She only noticed she was crying when the tears trickled down her neck.

Tomorrow it would all be over. He would go back to Iris, and she would stay behind, alone again.

She wanted Frans for herself. She wanted to share him with no-one. At the very thought of Iris, her mother, she experienced a violent jealousy, an emotion totally alien to her.

She fought her tears. Overwhelmed by emotion Frank sat down beside her on the couch kissing her tears away, whispering sweet nothings in her ear. "I love you, I love you, I'm crazy about you."

Suddenly a mad, inconceivable thought shot as a geyser into his feverish brain. *Would he tell her?* It was like jumping from an Olympic springboard: dizzying. In less than a minute Frans, in a fit of madness, revealed the black secret to his daughter. He was not her biological father. Iris and he had an 'open marriage' and Ciska was the child of another man.

In the face of her shattered expression Frans said, "Every disadvantage has its advantage, darling. Just like Woody Allen we can legally get married, be together forever." He told her about the DNA report, but as she definitely would want to see it he had little choice but to reveal that Hans was her biological father. "So, I have fucked both my fathers," escaped from her bloodless lips. "And mom fucked her own brother. What a mess!" Frans remained silent: he was too weak-kneed or too sensible to confess that he was to blame for the mess. Again the tears trickled down her ashen cheeks as she stared in the void for a long time.

*

In Hong Kong Frans had bought a harmonica bag for all the stuff he'd bought. Before his return trip everything had been carefully scrutinised to make sure no item could betray Ciska's presence. He had even emptied the contents of his wallet on a table and had checked every item before putting it back. *He was clean.* That he knew for sure. *Oh, if ever Iris would find out!* At 9 a.m. the hotel limousine was waiting. At 11.05 the Airbus took off.

**

As an Airbus technical consultant Frans had to go to Helsinki for a few days a week after his return. He couldn't find his passport.

Mild panic .It had to be somewhere, as he had passed customs at Schiphol Airport. Looking everywhere. All in vain. Iris helped finding it. She looked in the most improbable places, even at the bottom of the deep harmonica case. There she found a ticket from the drycleaners of the Manila Hotel with the name Mrs. Ciska van Gaal. She staggered, all went black, she had to clutch a chair to steady herself.

***

As always she kept mum about her discovery. Frans felt the Arctic atmosphere but didn't have a clue as to why. He knew she'd stopped loving him long ago. *Could this marriage still be saved?* The familiar refrain of women's magazines. One thing was for sure: The hurricane of the student ball had blown itself out long ago. What remained was a chilly spring breeze.

Iris had confronted Ciska with the ticket from the dry-cleaner's. Choking back tears and fury she said, "You're a slut. How dare you. With your own father!" Ciska, remarkably calm, had responded, "You're a slut. How dare you! With your own brother!" She walked over to her desk, extracted a copy of the DNA test from the drawer and threw it on the coffee table.

At that instant Iris' world collapsed.

She ran out of Ciska's apartment, jumped behind the wheel ant drove off at high speed towards Schiphol. At the towering windmill along freeway A4 she turned off to Hillegom. On the Leimuiderweg, a notorious two-lane road, her wing mirror hit an oncoming car. Her car, lurching drunkenly along the road, ended up in a ditch. Then everything went black. Wondrous to relate, Iris had only broken her left collar bone.

Epilogue

Iris had broken down completely. Depressed, hating herself, Frans and her daughter, she suffered from insomnia, anorexia, phobias and obsessional thoughts. Their friend, Roel, gynaecologist, had advised them to seek psychiatric help. At his recommendation they saw Dr. Jan Boeke, psychiatrist, who had published extensively on the recently discovered phenomena GSA, genetic sexual attraction.

When Frans and Iris during a joint visit learned for the first time about the GSA phenomenon, which had a direct bearing on the Hans-Iris relation because of the close physical correspondence, they were both surprised and - especially Iris - pleased. Now they understood - also from the examples Dr. Boeke presented - how strong the subconscious influences could be that contributed to this tragedy.

At the end of the third visit Dr. Boeke proposed cognitive behaviour therapy rather than psycho-analysis. He explained: "Not the problem itself, but the (wrong) thoughts are the cause of mental distress. By changing thinking the problems can be reduced and the patient relieved of his symptoms. Wrong thoughts lead to undesired emotions and dysfunctional behaviour."

Voilà, cognitive behaviour therapy in a nutshell. Thanks to the psychiatrist and the intelligence of the partners Frans and Iris quickly came to the clear understanding that here, apart from 'guilt and sexual abuse', other factors such as blind GSA and other influences were at play.

If Iris had not insisted long ago that he should sleep with Hans on the divan rather than with her, Frans sexual passion for Hans might have stayed dormant. Moreover, according to Dr. Bocke Frans sexual interest in Hans was at least for a large part the result of the close physical resemblance between Hans and Iris, a kind of side-effect of GSA, known as **shadow-GSA.**

After weekly sessions over a six-month period Iris' symptoms had virtually disappeared. Still, she was no longer the same woman as before, cheerful, spontaneous, extravert. Despite her clear understanding about her 'wrong thinking' and the psycho-biological forces involved, she continued to harbour a strong grudge against Frans and Ciska. As far as she was concerned the 'mother-daughter relation' had been permanently disrupted, despite her insight that the cause of their affair was the 'sexual itch' caused by androstenedione, coupled to other factors, such as Ciska's dislike of condoms, Frans' libertine mentality, etc. True, her anger was lessened by the psychiatrist observation: "Don't forget that your sex with Hans and Ciska's with Frans were due to desperation. In your case the desire for a child with Frans' genes, and with Ciska the urge to be rid of her 'sexual itch'." Despite her 'insight' Iris was completely fed up with Frans. **As far as she was concerned their marriage was over, permanently over.**

***

In the same period another far-reaching event had taken place. Sacha, Hans' wife, alarmed by what she had seen the evening she had forgotten her lipstick, had hired a private detective. As a result of this the sexual relation of Hans with both Frans and Iris came to light.

With oriental inscrutability she had remained silent, packed her bags and flown with Singapore Airlines to Kuala Lumpur**,** her city of birth, where she was welcomed by her parents with open arms.

Hans, initially devastated, sought and found comfort in the arms of his love, Iris, mutually connected by the bonds of GSA. In Iris, too, no longer plagued by guilt feelings towards Frans and Sacha, the mysterious forces of GSA flourished.

****

Hurricane **Frans** had blown itself out , Hurricane **Hans** raged and lifted Iris to heavenly bliss.

In London where she visited professor Arthur Wolf, GSA specialist, on the advice of her psychiatrist, Iris told him, "It's the most amazing sex I ever had. Don't ask me to give it up. I can't."

But the first amorous encounter since Iris and Hans were unattached was not stormy, but started cool. Their marriages had failed and now they were both clinging on to wreckage. Did they have a future? What would people say?

In the intimacy of the Holiday Inn room they didn't rush into each other's arms, but kept quiet at the beginning. Both were impressed by the gravity of this memorable moment: their freedom and at the same time their want of freedom. They spoke about their 'situation'.

When Hans said, "I'm crazy about you, but we have no future", she answered, "But I want to be with you."

Slowly his lips approached till halfway. Attracted, she bent over to him. They were sitting with only their faces touching, but more excitement flowed through their flesh than ever before.

*****

Frans married his stepdaughter Ciska during a simple ceremony attended only by the two witnesses, his brother and Ciska's best friend. They were honeymooning in Paris where they stayed at the 5-star Hotel Plaza-Athénéé.

Frans and Ciska walked into the bar of the Plaza when Frans spotted Woody Allen and Soon-Yi, his wife (and step-daughter) sitting on a stool, holding hands, Woody's head just jutting out above the bar. He was in Paris for the shooting of his latest film. Impulsively Frans grabbed Ciska's hand and seated himself next to Woody Allen. Thanks to Ciska's beauty and bubbly personality they were soon engaged in a lively conversation. The ice was broken when Frans told them they - he and his stepdaughter - were on their honeymoon. Ciska, didn't say much, but observed all the more. Woody was indeed as ugly as Woody, and Soon-Yi as Soon-Yi. But she was very nice.

After his fourth vodka Frans became philosophical. "To be or not to be that's the question," he quoted. Woody looked dumb.

"I don't know what the question is, but sex is definitely the answer." Woody declared, picking a nut. Frans, in an expansive mood, said, "You got a fine brain, Woody. I like that." "My brain is my second favourite organ." A bit woozy, Frans mumbled, kissing Ciska on her cheek, "Nothing beats love, right darling?" Woody disagreed.

"Sex alleviates tension, love causes it, "he observed. Woody thought Ciska was older, twenty-one, instead of barely eighteen. "Yes," Frans said, not without some pride, "she is a very mature girl."

Woody thought Soon-Yi was very immature. "Basically, my wife is very immature. I would be at home in my bath and she would come in and sink all my boats." Frans and Ciska had the evening of their life and Woody had been so charmed by Ciska's looks and charisma that he offered her a supporting part in his film. Ciska, just graduated from the school of acting, the *Theater School* in Amsterdam accepted eagerly.

******

A year later Ciska gave birth to their first child, a girl. After the rift with Iris Frans saw Hans only very occasionally, for Hans had to swear on the Holy Bible to break off all contact. After the birth of his daughter Frans decided to put a stop to it once and for all. He loved perversion, that was the fun part. But since he had become dad again he thought differently. *Sex with the grandfather of your child? That's really over the top!*

The dénouement

Shortly after Paris the final conversation took place between Frans and his psychiatrist, Dr. Boeke, who had treated both Frans and Iris, mostly in separate sessions. Dr. Boeke, bound by his oath of secrecy, had gained the trust of both parties and was completely familiar with all aspects and developments of this family tragedy. Part of his analysis is relevant to our story.

According to Dr. Boeke Iris had made up her mind to put an end to her erotic relationship with Hans once the condom sex to get pregnant was over. This despite the fact that she admitted that she had fallen in love with Hans as a result of the condom sex. Her strong will, sense of values, the fear that the crush would degenerate into sexual addiction, and last but not least, the fact that incest is considered a 'mortal sin' by the Catholic Church which makes it impossible to receive holy communion, made it highly improbable that Iris would ever have allowed herself to have intercourse with her brother again.

The cat among the pigeons was the testosterone injection Frans gave her under the pretext of a vitamin B12 injection.

As a result of the hormonally aroused intense libido and 'male shamelessness' Iris, in this critical period, fell victim to her carnal desires, reinforced by the magnetic attraction of GSA. This month-long period of unrestrained sexual licence and - what Iris called - 'sexual infatuation', had been fatal. The erotic 'addiction' had become a fact and had wiped away everything else. But the testosterone made another victim: Ciska.

Because Iris got pregnant from her brother as a result of a miscalculation or a freak of nature (too early ovulation resulting from super excitement) the development of the foetus was affected by the injected testosterone. This resulted in the foetus' ovaries producing too much of the normally present weak androgenic hormone androstenedione, the cause of Ciska's 'sexual itch problem'.

Without this problem she would never have had sex with Hans as her 'stallion' and so Frans could never have taken over Hans role when he left for Dubai for an extended period.

"In summary," Dr. Boeke said, lighting his pipe for the umpteenth time, "without the Estandron injection you would never have married Ciska and your marriage to Iris, though badly taxed, would have endured. Well, Mr. Van Gaal, you told me you're very happy with your step-daughter, Ciska, but realize full well that you owe everything to that one injection, in my opinion a criminal act."

As a psychiatrist he should never have made this last remark.